CW00324467

A Fatal Delusion

By the same author

Out of Bounds

A Fatal Delusion

A NOVEL

Frances Hill

JOHN MURRAY

© Frances Hill 1989

First published 1989
by John Murray (Publishers) Ltd
50 Albemarle Street, London W1X 4BD

Typeset by Rowland Phototypesetting Ltd
Bury St Edmunds, Suffolk
Printed in Great Britain
at the University Press, Cambridge

British Library Cataloguing in Publication Data
is available

ISBN 0-7195-4718-0

For Leon and Tamarin

Chapter One

BEATTIE swung the car through the gap in the trees and drove quickly uphill. The branches spanning the driveway almost cut out the sky. After the bright sun on the road it seemed dark as dusk. But Beattie did not slow down. She drove over detonating gravel up the last, steepest part of the rise and out from the woodland.

She had reached the level expanse of cleared, landscaped ground where her house was, high on the hill, surrounded by sky. She stopped in front of the garage. Heat broke over the roof, poured in through the windows and drenched her. She quickly gathered her sun-hat and bag from the passenger seat, clambered out and made for the building.

As she walked across the wide gravel area towards the

flower garden split into various levels by low stone embankments she noticed, not for the first time that week, that one or two bushes were in advanced need of pruning. After a momentary pause she turned back. She would collect gardening gloves, secateurs and the knife from the garage and set to at once. She had several hours unexpectedly free. Normally she would wait in New Dartmouth while Melly, her ten-year-old daughter, was having her dance class and then bring her back home. But that morning a friend had offered to pick Melly up from the class with her own daughter, keep her the rest of the morning, give her lunch and return her. The heat made the prospect of labour outside less than enticing. At nine-thirty, however, it should not yet be unbearable.

But before reaching the garage Beattie caught a glimpse, from her eye's corner, off to one side, of someone or something not there before. She turned her head quickly. A figure stood in the small patch of shadow under the porch. The immediate question of how it had got there brought fear. There was no car in the drive but for Beattie's. No one walked in that landscape. The endless New England expanses of seemingly free, wild country were tied up in parcels, sealed not by fences but custom and law. The ethos of each for himself ran deep and strong. Tracts of earth, portions of humankind's planet, were private as bedrooms. There were few footpaths, no freely-walked edges of fields, no open hillsides, no riverbank towpaths, no sheeptracks or cowtracks. The land could be stared at from sundecks and fast-moving cars, not entered, explored, mixed into the soul.

The figure stepped forward into the sunlight. It was a woman, quite tall, in a shirt over shorts.

'Beattie!'

The woman moved with long, rapid strides, almost running. Beattie was gripped by a sense of dislike. Recognition followed a half-second later. It was induced by the pear shape and the ungraceful motion and the singular sheen. Even judging by local high standards the woman's hair, skin and nails had been brought to an extraordinary polish. This was Elizabeth Andersen, Beattie's neighbour, a few years Beattie's junior. Beattie now noticed, as she came closer, that her perfection was marred. She looked, for the first time Beattie could ever remember, as though she felt hot. A lock of the thick, expensively styled brown crop hung apart from the rest, over an eyebrow. A shirt button, half way down, had worked its way free.

'Hi, Beattie! I was looking for you, you must be wondering, seeing me here . . . How are you? Gee, it's gotten so warm. You look great . . .' Elizabeth stood awkwardly, one knee still bent, toe pointed, re-aligning the stray lock with long fingers. Her words, though distracted and breathless, were full of her customary tone of inauthentic enthusiasm. But her blue eyes, as they gazed into Beattie's, showed no feeling. Their blue seemed the original concentrate, left undiluted. It was the colour of the high summer New England sky. This on hot cloudless days seemed always to Beattie solid and impenetrable. The same blue in Elizabeth's eyes made them appear just as opaque. They seemed not in the slightest like windows – more like small, brilliant shields.

'You gave me a fright.'

'Gee, did I? I'm sorry.' Elizabeth laughed, in that way she had, with no connection with humour. 'I came to ask you and Bob to dinner tonight? I couldn't get you on the phone?' She made these statements as though they were questions. Her smile, showing bright, even teeth, was full of the same clockwork zest as her voice.

'How did you *get* here? Where's your car?' Beattie's accent might have been thought a cruel take-off of Elizabeth's. But its over-emphasised quality was in fact due to her having adopted it, as camouflage, on arrival from England. She had had a career as an actress before giving birth to her daughter. It had been neither an amazing success nor a stark failure. But she slipped easily from one 'voice' to another.

Elizabeth shifted her eyes. Her smile dissolved.

'I walked.'

'You *walked*?'

Beattie stared in amazement. 'You walked here from your house? All the way? In this heat?'

Elizabeth's eyes stayed averted. Beattie kept staring, stunned out of normal politeness. She scanned the Nordic American face, with its good bones and the extremely blue eyes, and the somewhat full body. The tanned skin glistened slightly but was otherwise flawless. The eye make-up was intact. The clothes were tidy, apart from the button. Beattie suddenly noticed a very small cut on Elizabeth's leg. There was a bubble of blood on the calf, the size of a pinhead, and beneath it a short, drying trickle. She felt a small, quick sensation of pleasure, not at Elizabeth's pain, if there had been any, but at the sight of a flaw. She next noticed that Elizabeth's sandals, and the long feet inside them, were smeared with dirt. Elizabeth was, it seemed, telling the truth. Yet there was in her manner an appearance of falsity different in kind, with a cause more specific, than her normal strange artifice.

Elizabeth renewed eye contact. Her expression revived. She regained her air of assurance.

'I thought I'd try your suggestion, Beattie?'

'What suggestion?'

'About finding a trail through our land onto yours?'

'Did I suggest that?'

'You said you might try it some day. I wanted to jump the gun and surprise you. I thought, Beattie'll be so astonished, when I arrive without the Toyota.'

'Well, you're right, I am astonished. I thought you never walked anywhere.'

'When you talked about finding that trail I decided it sounded a real fun thing to try.'

'I don't remember . . .'

'You see, Beattie, you're introducing to us lazy Americans your wonderful English way of walking places.'

Beattie felt an expression of instinctive distaste come over her face before she could stop it. But Elizabeth gave no sign of noticing. Her attention had wandered: she was glancing down over her person, checking her clothes.

4

Beattie suddenly guessed she rarely spotted the half-hidden meanings in glances or words. Perhaps she was content with a view of the world that assumed others' inner lives to be much like her own. Perhaps she was not fully aware they existed.

Beattie said, 'I'd no idea I was so influential.'

Elizabeth was re-fastening the mutinous button. When she had finished she straightened her shirt and looked up. She said, 'Beattie, I know it's short notice but *could* you and Bob come on over tonight? This morning I suddenly thought, I'd *love* to see Beattie and Bob, it was one of those whims . . .'

Her tone had moved into that variant of her customary manner that was startlingly, instead of just mildly, patronising. She gave one of her brief, pointless laughs.

'I know Bob's away till tonight but I thought maybe you're expecting him back home for dinner?'

Beattie had remarked to herself, when she first met her, that Elizabeth carried on a lot of the time as though she were royalty. American royalty. Perhaps a Kennedy sister or daughter. There seemed an assumption of unquestionably superior looks, grace and manners – if not, in Elizabeth's case, wealth and prestige. Though, in these respects too, she must have believed her claims were not inconsiderable, at least in New Dartmouth. Out of her hearing, Beattie could laugh at her. But in her presence she often felt helplessly angry at being so patronised. Sometimes, as now, she rebelled. She had fine-tuned her instinct for doing so over the months. She now embarked on a series of movements which she knew to be stagily graceful. They included tilting the hips, bending the waist, raising and twisting the thin arms and shoulders and waving and turning the hands. The ostensible object of all these manoeuvres was to put on her hat. By the time she had done so she had without question gained the advantage. Elizabeth shifted her large, sandalled feet, looking away. Beattie gazed at her from under the wide, wavy brim, knowing full well that the hat was unusually flattering, the look on her face all enquiring innocence.

'Since you couldn't get me on the phone, what made you think I'd be here when you came?'

Elizabeth resorted again to the tactic of fixing her eyes but blinked more than usual. She smiled but not as widely as normal. Her tone, when she spoke, had a slight edge of what sounded like nervous aggression.

'I figured maybe you were out working in your wonderful garden.'

'You could have called later.'

'Sure I could, but I liked the idea of finding that trail.'

'But didn't you know I take Melly to dance class on Saturday mornings? I recall discussing her class with you.'

Elizabeth made a movement expressing impatience, perhaps even displeasure. She muttered 'no', looking away. But in a moment she recovered and met Beattie's eye and gave a smile closer than before to the full-scale version.

'What about tonight, Beattie? Can you come?'

Despite the smile, Beattie thought she detected a distinct lack of enthusiasm for the possibility of her invitation's being accepted. Indeed, a hope of refusal. The cranked-up zest had almost run down. Why on earth, Beattie wondered, had Elizabeth extended the invitation at all? She could think of no possible reason. She could not for a moment believe that Elizabeth had felt an urgent desire to see them.

Beattie considered what she should do. She felt no need to rush her decision. Elizabeth had chosen to walk here. She must have plenty of time at her disposal this morning. She weighed up the factors. Bob would want to go very much. He was extremely, even extraordinarily, gregarious. She knew he would want to go out to dinner despite having been away from home for a week. And then going out would save her shopping and cooking. On the other hand, she would have to find a baby-sitter for Melly or a place for her to stay overnight. And she would have to spend several hours in Dick and Elizabeth's company. But on hearing the plan Bob would enter an instant good mood, which might last the weekend. She would not have much of a chance to talk to him by himself till tomorrow. Still, they would then have all day.

Elizabeth's apparent reluctance to receive them was not at all a deterrent to going. Rather the opposite. She had, for whatever mysterious reason, ventured the offer. She must put up as best as she might with its being accepted. It was perhaps this thought that made up Beattie's mind for her.

'I guess we can. Thanks a lot. What time would you like us?'

'Eight.'

'O.K. Bob should be home by then. He said seven. If he rings to say he'll be late I'll tell him he can't be.'

'You do that, Beattie. Tell him we'll be mad as hell if he doesn't make it on time.'

There was a pause.

'D'you want to drop in for iced tea or coffee or something?'

There was another hiatus. A short one.

'I'm fine.'

Did that mean she didn't? Neither woman made any move. It occurred to Beattie that Elizabeth expected to be offered a lift back to her house. Her enthusiasm for the wonderful old English way of walking places was no doubt exhausted. For a moment Beattie felt she'd be damned if she'd get back into the hot car to chauffeur Elizabeth home. She hadn't wanted or asked her to come on this mad expedition. But then she remembered the invitation to dinner that evening. That created some obligation.

'I'll drive you home.'

'No, it's O.K. I'll walk back.'

'That's absurd.'

'I'll be fine.'

Beattie lowered her eyes, with some fluttering of eyelash, to the smudge on Elizabeth's leg, where the bubble had burst and smeared into the trickle.

'You might get more cuts and scratches.'

Elizabeth glanced down. She had known the blemish was there, Beattie could see, but had forgotten about it. Just for the moment. She looked annoyed and, Beattie thought, slightly anxious.

'It's nothing.'

'I suppose most of the walk was over open land? In fact I wouldn't have thought you'd need to go through forest at all. I'll come round the back of the house with you and you can point out your route. I'd be interested to see it.'

'I guess perhaps I'll go back by the road.' Elizabeth gestured, in the direction suggested. As she did so, Beattie noticed a raw, scraped, bloodied patch on the palm of her hand.

'Oh, my goodness, look at your hand. It's cut to ribbons. Jeepers. It *must* have been hard getting through.'

Elizabeth looked down at her palm, more disconcerted than Beattie had seen her. 'It's nothing. A couple of scratches.'

'And the other one . . .' That, Beattie had spotted, was in the same state. 'Jeez . . . Come in and wash them.'

Beattie stepped towards the house. But Elizabeth failed to follow.

'I'd really rather get home.' Elizabeth now seemed rather seriously upset. She seemed angry.

'All right. As you like.'

Elizabeth, recovering her composure a little, met Beattie's eye for, by her standards, an unusually short moment. Then she turned, saying in a low, hurried mutter, 'See you tonight.' She set off at a very good pace over the gravel, looking slightly ungainly, the inelegant width of her waist and rump clearly in evidence. She had soon disappeared, down the slope of the drive, into the forest.

Beattie felt suddenly angry at having accepted. Bob had been away for a week. They had a great deal to talk about. As the time had worn on she had felt less and less satisfied with his explanation – of being short-handed and busy – for staying away for so long. She had become convinced there was trouble.

Beattie wanted time to bring up this subject with due care and tact, to discuss it at leisure, to re-introduce it when

Bob had veered off onto some other topic without making him angry.

She pictured her husband, his body large and running to fat, the expression on his square, red, handsome face unresponsive and mulish. She felt angry with him and herself and Elizabeth.

And, besides, what was Elizabeth up to? She wanted to discuss that with Bob too.

She could probably arrange for Melly to stay overnight with the friend she had been with that morning. But tomorrow she would be back home by lunchtime. Bob would sleep until then. He was always exhausted at the end of the week. She longed now for the time alone with her husband that she could have had, had she said 'no' to Elizabeth.

Chapter
Two

*B*OB's car seemed to be steering itself. It knew the way
perfectly. It bounced and swayed in the rivers of traffic,
made several right-angled turns, braked abruptly at sudden
impediments. Minor roadworks appeared without warning
beyond double-parked vans; yellow taxis tossed out their
passengers, like unwanted ballast, yards from shore; wierdly
dressed, confused, often apparently stark mad pedestrians
stepped into the flow. The car stopped at a light, swinging on
high well away from the currents. Then it jolted again
through the streams squeezed to turbulent closeness by the
sheer concrete mountains forming their banks. At last it shot
out at speed to an avenue, straight and broad, to move
quickly and smoothly en route to the north, and swung itself
to the left onto the highway that led to New Dartmouth and
home.

Bob himself seemed part of the mechanism. A single small section of brain was detached and apart from the contemporary centaur – man and car, not man and horse – that drove up the highway. That section worked quickly and boldly, knowing its strength. It was seeking solutions to what would have looked, to any impartial observer, insoluble problems. Success was turning to failure like a palace of marble changing to ice and dissolving. But Bob believed there must be some means somehow, though he did not know yet what it could be, of reversing the process.

Somewhere subsumed in the centaur, hidden away from the brain that was busily thinking, there was terror.

Cash flow was the nub. Bob's business, like many before it, had expanded too quickly. Bob was keen to make money but without the true businessman's obsession with that single goal. He was distracted by hopes of achieving something of real social worth that would add to humanity's knowledge and goodness and pleasure. He was also over-impatient for rapid success. He had broken the first rule in the business school's book. He had let the firm grow unchecked with the demand for its products. His imagination and cleverness in giving his small publishing business sudden new impetus looked like proving his downfall.

The highway transformed itself quickly and easily from a bridge stretched on high above concrete and asphalt and the edge of the river to a ledge in the side of a hill, an almost sheer bluff reaching up on the right, disappearing in trees, a long drop on the left. It was approaching the high northern shore of the island, lofty at one end, sloping to flatness, tapering to a point, made over in parts during two hundred years into what its inhabitants knew as simply the City.

The ledge widened. The car stopped and Bob tossed some quarters into the beak of the money machine on his left. The wooden arm in front of him lifted and he passed through the toll.

As the car drove itself over the bridge off the top of the rock Bob's attention was caught as always by the sight of the rivers below, broad as lakes, flowing into each other. This crossing seemed as ever a flight and escape. To have to go back to the City to live, to the apartment in which he and Beattie had once lived full-time but was now a mere *pied à terre*, would mean the end of his hopes. It was too appalling a prospect for him to dwell on for long.

From the crest of the bridge the rivers and the long strips of shore seemed to stretch an extraordinary distance to the purple horizon. Bob found himself thinking of all the people way down there beneath him. The idea grew in his mind until, with a God-like perspective, he envisioned the millions strewn over the landmass.

The sentence 'They're all searching' appeared in his thoughts fully formed. An image came into his mind of the graves of some of his forebears on the side of a steep, stony hill, seen twelve years before. The fading of bloodlines to limitless distance seemed compelling and strange. But he could no sooner go to the west coast of Ireland to live than back to the City. His hopes were all in his new house and land. He foresaw an existence in that beautiful landscape of wealth and success. He would expand his business, social activities, pastimes and pleasures. His life would be rich and complete. As he remembered the threat to these hopes he felt fear.

But his spirits lifted, as always, as he reached the far shore, and the panic melted away.

The landmarks heralding his journey's end – the picnic facility, the Marbury service station, the Sanders Inn restaurant – slid into consciousness under figures and deadlines and dates and stirred new ideas. Bob saw a large, wooden structure, surrounded by sky, aglow in the sunlight. The house had been formed from two barns by the previous owners and in its simple elegance seemed to him perfect. He had adored it when he first saw it, a year and a half ago, but loved it even more now he owned it.

He saw his daughter running towards him, bulky but with shining dark hair like her mother's and clear hazel eyes. Beattie came into view just behind her, head held high, smiling. She wore her wide skirt and a suntop. But instead of keeping on walking she faded and then re-appeared in what Bob knew without thinking about it, as one knows where one is in a dream, was the kitchen. She was for some reason kneeling. The skirt was spread round her, the suntop showing smooth-skinned expanses of shoulder and back. He realised he was remembering a moment from the weekend before. She was taking a cake or loaf from the oven. Her hair was up in a bun, her neck slim and bare; she looked round towards him, eyes dark and quick. Remembrance was suddenly wholly abandoned and he was plunged deep in a hard porn home movie, ripping the suntop, slamming the door of the oven back shut, fondling the breasts, shoving the skirt up to the waistband, tearing the familiar pink knickers, knocking the loaf to one side with his elbow, removing his trousers, grasping his arms round the slim hips and thighs and thrusting himself into her with extraordinary gusto.

Bob braked at a light, a little too sharply. He wondered what on earth had come over him. My God, he reflected, this is absurd. It's embarrassing. It's perverted. We've been married twelve years.

Yet the mood did not pass. Some inner projectionist kept showing pictures of Beattie, fully or partially clothed or not clothed at all; in various moods, all enticing: mischievous; humorous; a little aroused; downright randy. All the slides showed her slimness and straightness of line, slender neck, neat wrists and hands, which Beattie knew very well how to show to advantage and use to effect. Beattie was not classically beautiful nor even specially pretty. Her face was too thin: it could look haggard and sallow. More often it seemed neither handsome nor plain. But when Beattie was enjoying herself, specially when talking and laughing, her dark eyes and olive skin and thin face seemed enticing. She had a mole on one cheek, near the temple, which was transformed at such moments from a blemish to something alluring. When she was made up and becomingly dressed and in a good mood few women appeared more desirable. So it seemed to her husband. Her body and face were the natural equivalents of someone whose simple attire is transformed by her stunning accessories.

Bob now saw her spreadeagled, nude, on their bed, the delicate bones apparent at shoulders and hips under a layer of just the right thickness of smooth-textured flesh. A new erotic home movie seemed about to start rolling.

But then, instead, into and over these thoughts came a darkness. That apparently un-aging figure, on a woman in her late thirties who had once borne a child, was no mere unsought blessing. It was achieved by the coercion of the animal self into not wanting food. She would deny feeling hunger. She would scarcely eat, sometimes, for days. The shadow over Bob's feelings was spreading: the sense of that conquest of need so intrinsic and crucial to Beattie's emotional being led into half-conscious awareness of other dark places . . . He pictured her, distant, sharp-eyed and judging, her erotic appeal gone completely.

'At times I've wanted to kill her.'

The thought dispelled the miasma. Bob could then, in a spirit of calm curiosity, ask himself whether in any conceivable circumstances he could take Beattie's life. He wondered whether he could possibly do so if he found her naked in bed with a man. He tried to picture the scene. But his heart was not in it. Nothing convincing appeared in the way of nude bodies or disarranged bedclothes. No feelings were stirred. Despite all his love for her he could never experience such violent jealousy.

As the car drove on through New Dartmouth Bob kept pondering the subject of killing. Would he have shot Black and Tans during Easter, 1916? He would surely have fought and killed in the war against Hitler. But was he capable of cold-blooded murder, out of hatred or fear? There would have to be a terrible lack inside someone, he thought with sudden, clear insight, to cause them to kill.

Chapter Three

'*SHE* was poking about,' Beattie said.

'What?'

'I'm almost certain Elizabeth Andersen was poking about before I arrived. I found the studio door open.'

The two of them sat on the patio. Bob had showered and changed and was ready to leave for the Andersens when it was time.

'Maybe you're right, perhaps she had a look round. Does it matter?'

'You know I can't bear *anyone* seeing my pictures when they're not finished. But it didn't look as though she'd touched anything.'

'I should forget it then, Beattie.'

'I hate the idea of her in there.'

'It's not important.'

What a fuss about nothing, Bob thought. If only she knew. He felt his panic surge to the surface. He put down his drink and took a large handful of twiglets and nuts from the bowl near his elbow and crammed them into his mouth. The panic waned. He felt glad he had told her nothing so far. He might well never have to. He was sure to find a solution. He rubbed his fingers together to rid them of crumbs.

Beattie was seated across from him at the white garden table, dressed for the dinner party in a new white frilly blouse and straight, dark blue skirt. She had her 'going-out' face on: the eyes bigger, darker and brighter, skin smoother, shape neater, than for ordinary life. Her cheeks seemed slim and sleek instead of too thin. The mole up near her temple had now a coquettish appearance. The new visage had been already in place when he came home. She had not let him kiss her except for a brushing of lips, for fear of smudging it, though they had hugged closely for a minute or two when he entered the house. The time before he could take her to bed stretched ahead like a gaol sentence.

'I'm sure the studio door was shut when I left here this morning.'

'Perhaps she looked in thinking you were engrossed in your painting.' Bob reached for his drink. 'Deaf to the world.' He drained most of the glass.

'Such a thing wouldn't occur to Elizabeth Andersen. There's nothing under that pricey hairdo apart from plots of soaps and shopping lists and names she's planning to drop.' Beattie lowered her drink to her lap, in tacit protest at the Hogarthian swig she had just had to witness. Her left hand joined her right in holding the glass as though to prevent it escaping back up to chest level.

'I suspect there's quite a lot *buried*.'

'There's sure not much on the surface.'

'There'd be plenty wouldn't agree.'

'What d'you mean?'

'Whatever you think of her, she's generally thought to be very attractive.'

'Do *you* think she's very attractive?'

'No, not really. She's too plastic for me. I like real flesh, with sweat glands and pores.'

'Thank you, my darling.'

'And I don't much like her manner.'

'Patronising.'

'I don't like being gushed over.'

'I just *adore* that tie, Bob. Did you get it in London? It's so *English*.'

'Right.'

'You're so *handsome*, Bob, honey.'

'No. She'd never . . .' Bob paused for a moment, 'come on as strong as that.' After another brief pause he went on, 'She wouldn't use the word "honey". She never uses endearments at all. Not even to Dick.'

'Not even? *Specially* not to poor Dick.'

'Yeah.'

'Mind you,' Beattie said, 'she may seem simple and boring but she's done some strange things in her life.'

'Such as?'

'She worked in a zoo once.'

'How d'you know?'

'She told me. Can you imagine Elizabeth Andersen mucking out elephant cages?'

'Perhaps she stood around in a swimsuit in charge of the dolphins. That seems more her style.'

'As far as I'm concerned whatever she did it's a *big* count against her. She should try being locked in a cage for a while.' Beattie removed one hand from the glass and raised her drink to her mouth, took a small sip, then brought it down again to her lap. 'Another thing I've heard is that she hasn't been too good lately about paying her bills.'

'But they're rolling in money.'

'Lack of cash isn't the problem. She's just slow getting round to signing the cheques. She's not coping too well with that gallery either. It's closed half the time. She's losing *masses* of custom. You see *droves* of would-be shoppers in New Monmouth High Street getting back in their cars.'

'A slight exaggeration.'

'Only slight.'

Beattie fell silent.

Bob's thoughts went back to his business. He felt another sharp twist of fear. He gulped the last of his drink and turned his mind quickly to practical details. He was soon mentally busy with sums.

Beattie half turned in her chair to gaze at the view over the wide stretch of land, mostly cleared, with woods down on the left and off in the distance. The low rays of the sun slanted across it, giving a glow to the patio wall, above the sheer drop down the mountain.

She said suddenly, 'That's their chimney stack.'

'Where?'

'Look.' She pointed. 'That grey patch sticking out from the top of the trees. Way over there.'

It took Bob a while to see it. He leant forward and shielded his eyes with his hand.

'Yeah, you're right, it must be, it can't be anything else.'

'*Look* at that distance. She had to find her own way. *And* push through the forest. Her hands were covered in scratches. She had a cut on her leg. *Elizabeth Andersen.*' Beattie paused for a moment, then went on, sounding anxious, 'Anyway *why* did she push through the forest? She could have got here over the fields.'

Bob put his empty glass down on the table. 'She hadn't thought it out properly. She came here on an impulse.'

'Hell.'

'What's the matter?'

'I wish we weren't going there.'

'Oh, come on, maybe they'll invite some of those famous directors and movie stars she says she's such friends with.'

'Not a chance. It'll be just us, I know it. Look, go without me. Say I felt ill.'

'Beattie! That's so unlike you.'

'I can't face her.'

'Did she say or do something you haven't told me about?'

'No.' Beattie rose from her seat. 'It's funny, though, it's such a strong feeling, this not wanting to go.' She walked round the table. 'It's kind of like *dread*. It's bizarre.'

Bob reached up his hand, she took it and he pulled her down on his lap. She lay her head on his wide chest and he hugged her.

'You're being real strange.'

'Yeah, I know. I *feel* strange. I've never liked her but this not wanting to go there is different.'

'What can she do to you?'

'Nothing, I guess.'

'Look, you can't back out now. We want to stay on good terms with them.'

'Do we?'

'Sure we do. Why not?'

Beattie half turned on his lap.

'I hate it when you're away a whole week.'

'Mmmm.'

'D'you need to do that again?'

Bob shifted slightly in his chair, tipping Beattie an inch or two but then pulling her towards him and gripping her even more tightly.

'I hope not.'

She looked up at him.

'Is the business in trouble, Bob?'

He relaxed his hold.

'It is,' she said.

'Not really.'

'You're going to have to tell me about it. Did you imagine you weren't?'

'There's no point, Bea. All you'd do is worry and there's nothing to worry about.'

'That's absurd. I don't worry unnecessarily. You know that perfectly well. You always say I like taking risks.'

'When I come home here I want to forget about it.'

After a pause she intoned, in her native, standard

English accent, '"Dwell I but in the suburbs of your good pleasure? If it be no more, Portia is Brutus' harlot, not his wife . . ."'

'O.K.'

'Then he says . . .'

'You needn't mount a production.'

'You have to tell me what's happening.'

'I will.'

'When?'

'Sometime.'

'When?'

'Very soon.'

'When?'

'Tomorrow.'

'Promise?'

'Yes, Bea, I promise.'

'D'you remember what Brutus says?'

'Not offhand.'

'"You are my true and honourable wife, as dear to me as are the ruddy drops that visit my sad heart."'

'I'd have said the same if I happened to have thought of it.'

'I know you would, darling.' Beattie hugged him tightly. He kissed her hair.

She let go and stood up.

'I'm going to have to go, aren't I?'

'Sure you are.' Bob looked at his watch. 'Time to leave.'

Chapter Four

'YOU look great, Beattie.' Elizabeth was holding open the door of her house and smiling intently, eyes and teeth at their hugest and brightest. 'What an *adorable* blouse.'

'Thank you, Elizabeth.' Beattie managed a fair-sized smile and passed into the corridor. As she glanced back she saw Elizabeth coquettishly inclining her head as she looked towards Bob. He was also tilting his head, as well as grinning in a way that looked to Beattie rather inane. This followed his initial wide-eyed reaction, when Elizabeth appeared, of what Beattie had spotted at once was surprised sexual pleasure. Elizabeth passed her again as they all moved towards the living room. As she was turned slightly away, opening the door, Beattie quickly and covertly looked her over.

She wore a low-cut, tight dress, flared at the hips into a shortish, full skirt. It was flattering to an extent that was for Elizabeth extremely unusual. She did not normally clothe herself with particular flair. It was exactly her eye colour and caused a compelling impression that a few drops more of blue concentrate had been dropped in her pupils. It managed to produce a deep cleavage from an average-sized bust. The shortness and shape of the skirt, aided by the spindly high heels on a pair of gleaming blue sandals, emphasised the chunky but not at all unattractive curves of the legs. There was now no sign of the cut. It had healed quickly. Or it had perhaps been disguised by whatever it was that had brought up a polish all over the skin.

Smooth tanned fingers finished in high gloss pink nails. One or two small strips of band aid, Beattie spotted, adhered to the palms. But they did not cover entirely the scratched and raw areas.

'Come on in. It's a mess, I'm afraid.' She laughed. 'It's been one thing after another today. I just *love* giving dinner parties. But I always end by doing far more than I meant to and then I only just get it all finished in time?' Elizabeth's statement unexpectedly ended up as a question. She stood, holding the doorhandle. She switched her smile from Beattie to Bob and then, after momentarily holding Bob's gaze, back to Beattie.

'Morey's didn't have any sea bass so I went on to the Betta Price. I got stuck behind one of those slow-moving trucks and you know how when that happens that road's so narrow and twisting you can't pass all the way down? As my very best friend Judy Walsh said to me recently you don't think of the time it'll take Liz till afterwards.' (Judy Walsh was an actress of moderate fame who had a house in the area. Beattie was startled by this reference to her as 'very best friend'. Elizabeth had not only never mentioned her before in this capacity but had never before mentioned her. The most recent previous 'very best friend' had been the youngish wife of an aging but still crowd-pulling film star.) 'It's my favourite fish, it's fabulous, I had it not long ago at

Dick Rolph's.' (Dick Rolph was a photographer of equally moderate fame to that of Miss Walsh.) 'So incredibly talented.'

'The sea bass?'

Beattie could not resist this.

Elizabeth gave a laugh rather different from usual. It expressed the customary pretended amusement but also some genuine uncertainty.

She muttered, 'I meant Dick Rolph.' Then she turned and led the way through the door to the living room.

Once they were inside she glanced round, quite re-covered it seemed, and re-lit the smile.

'Here we are. Now you must both make yourselves comfortable. We're going to be very informal tonight. There's no one else coming. I asked Judy but she was just leaving to go down to the City.'

There was no sign of the mess of which she had warned them. The only item which might perhaps be invoked as not in its preordained place was the *New Dartmouth Examiner* which lay on the arm of a chair. Elizabeth crossed over to it at once, picked it up, folded it quickly though not very neatly and tucked it under her bare, smoothly tanned arm.

'Dick'll be along in a minute. He's still in the shower. Let me get you a drink. Sit down anywhere.' Elizabeth, with the paper still held tight to her side, moved about the room as she spoke, in a manner assured but ungainly, glancing at sofas and chairs as though she were checking them for any developments since she last looked them over. She came to a halt, after covering much of the floorspace, at a capacious armchair, upholstered all over in yellow, facing the window. 'Bob, why not go here, you'll have the view, not that you can see much any more, I'm afraid, it's got almost dark. Beattie, you go on the couch, I'll join you when I've fixed us our drinks.'

Beattie and Bob sat down as instructed.

Beattie was very aware that Bob was engaged in what she always thought of as 'goggling'.

She felt this word described better than 'ogling' or

'leering' Bob's facial expression on occasions when he felt the force of an unforeseen sexual attraction. His eyes gave the impression of bulging a little. The large mouth seemed a touch pursed. The result on the broad, ruddy visage was a boyish salaciousness, eager and yearning.

Beattie wished, not for the first time in their twelve years of marriage, that he knew how to make his responses to unlooked-for sexual stimuli less blatantly obvious. Underlying that wish was another: that those responses themselves were less wholly predictable. She often felt the need to remind herself that she had only got what she ought to have reckoned on in marrying an Irish American Catholic. And, what was more, an Irish American Catholic who had at one moment intended himself for the priesthood. She was paying now for the intense romantic excitement at the start of their marriage of awakening and satisfying first, full sexual love in a strongly emotional and sensuous nature.

Bob, as he had stated earlier that evening, did not customarily find Elizabeth Andersen specially attractive. However, the intensified eye colour and cleavage had all too clearly made a strong impact.

This was painful. Half an hour ago Elizabeth had been an object of suspicion and even scorn to them both. Now Bob had abandoned this united perspective, for one she could not possibly share. Besides, earlier he had been ogling Beattie herself.

She felt doubly abandoned.

She wondered why Elizabeth showed no response to Bob's interest. To Beattie he seemed still, as he had when she married him, the most attractive man she had met in her life. If anything, his looks and charm had improved with the years. They were no longer those of a slim, handsome youth but of a powerful man in his prime. Right now, if you overlooked flaws such as specks on his jacket and a shortness of trouser showing goose pimpled calves, he looked wonderful. The glass of stiff gin he had drunk on the patio had ruddied his already strong-coloured complexion but had also brightened his eyes and enlivened his large, good-looking features. His hair had grown becomingly tousled as he massaged his scalp and twisted his curls.

He had honed his charm over the years to a sharp, subtle instrument. But he was fully aware that a free, open manner was a part of it and had carefully maintained that. Beattie believed he had done so instinctively but if he had needed to use conscious cleverness he undoubtedly would have.

Despite his air of ingenuousness she had been aware of something murky in Bob – a shadow over a part of his nature – as soon as she met him. Though she now knew him and the areas of darkness inside him so thoroughly she still had not fathomed that particular shade. To everyone else, she felt sure, it was invisible.

In any case, the looks and charm caused women caught unawares – waitresses, shopgirls, new acquaintances, even old friends after long separations – to look suddenly awkward or even to blush. When a woman was given his full and admiring attention she could almost always be seen to be considerably stirred. Beattie did not find this the least bit surprising. In her view so few men possessed anything pleasing about them that the sudden appearance of masculine attractiveness always came as a shock.

Yet Elizabeth seemed immune.

She had embarked on a discussion of what they should drink during which she swept round the room, picking up and putting down ashtrays and shaking and re-positioning what she, together with the rest of the American populace, referred to as pillows. Orders taken at last, she left by the door they had come through.

'They've altered the lighting,' Beattie observed.

'Have they?' Bob stared round with the surprised look he invariably wore when some visual change was referred to.

'Look, they've got that new lamp stand. With the purplish shade. It's giving a faint lilac glow to the bookcase.'

'Wasn't that there before?'

'No, of course not. I don't think it helps much.'

The room was the strangest Beattie had ever been in. As

was the house. It struck her each time with as much force as ever. The room, as was the house, was precisely octagonal. Dick, an architect, had designed it himself down to every last detail in shape, structure and, with a little help from Elizabeth, decor.

Three walls were of glass. In daylight they looked onto a lawn and several large trees and a good, though not spectacular, view. They now revealed merely the amorphous dark shapes of the trees and a glint of horizon. The wall opposite the central glass section held a huge, elaborate fireplace embellished with everything that could conceivably be constructed or found or adapted to embellish a fireplace: spit, fender, tongs; log-holder, toasting fork, poker; a mantelpiece covered with *objets*. The walls on each side were coated, from top to bottom, with books. The other two walls, as though transported from some club now presumably strangely denuded, were panelled with wood. The new lampshade stood near them, casting over the whole, as Beattie had said, a faint lilac glow.

Glancing across the room produced a feeling of strangeness, if not serious mental discomfort. One end, sparsely furnished, looking out on the garden and vista, seemed a room for breakfast or long northern evenings in summer, the other, dark and *gemütlich*, self-sufficient, full of warm, purple detail, for long winter nights. Perhaps Dick had intended just such a dichotomy. Beattie thought it wise on the whole not to ask him.

This curious room's chief creator now stood at what Beattie judged must be almost exactly its nub, poised between summer and winter, morning and evening. He seemed oddly still, staring forward, his legs slightly apart, his arms folded, looking almost as though he himself were some species of curious edifice, thrown up rather hurriedly but then placed in position with care as a centrepiece. He was wearing a flimsy, pale blue, open necked shirt, exposing a V at the neck of pink skin which looked mottled and tender, no doubt much given to sunburn and acne. He was facing the windows. His back regions, considerably crumpled in both shirt and trouser, were toward the huge, empty fireplace. He was tall and thin, of an unusual design, with a strangely flat torso. He looked notably stiff and unsupple. He made Beattie think of the Tin Man in *The Wizard of Oz*, slightly flattened. He seemed to bear in his body more tensions than one mere mortal frame could sustain. Though at this moment standing quite still he had a habit of moving his body and limbs without warning into all sorts of strange postures in an apparent attempt to relieve them of minor discomfort. His face, above the wide but thin chest and tender pink neck, was unexpectedly round. Having said his 'hi there's' and 'how are you's', he now stood strangely silent, his expression suggesting that he had suddenly sunk into deep contemplation of what could be seen of his land. He might have been considering the improvement or otherwise to the immediate prospect by the felling or planting of one or more trees. Or the building of an extension. Perhaps a second, miniature octagon, adjoining the first.

Beattie wondered if he and Elizabeth had just had a row, either in the usual way of hosts and hostesses minutes before the first guests' arrival or as the result of some genuinely serious conflict. Dick was often abstracted but not at moments when his attention was clearly required. He was usually eager to please. Bob and Beattie had met him and Elizabeth five or six times on social occasions since they had moved to New Dartmouth twelve months before: he had been always an assiduously amiable neighbour.

Elizabeth, having delivered the drinks, now appeared with a board on which sat several sorts and conditions of cheeses plus a startlingly large range of crackers. The American custom of producing a cheese board at the beginning rather than the end of a meal had struck Beattie at first as exceedingly strange. She was now entirely accustomed to it. But she always went to great lengths to avoid actually eating any of what was on offer.

Elizabeth placed the board on the low glass-topped table a foot or two from Bob's knees. She then handed him a folded pink paper napkin. Bob somehow simultaneously managed both to 'goggle' and to avert his eyes, looking abashed. Elizabeth, in response, exhibited a mild self-consciousness. But this seemed scarcely more than what she invariably displayed when she was looked at. She showed no other feeling. She might be flattered and pleased; she might not. When she departed Bob leaned forward at once, picked up a small knife and plate and cut a fair-sized hunk off what looked, from where Beattie was sitting, like Brie.

Beattie stared at this cheese with great interest. Whatever it was, it looked very runny. This was surprising. Brie, Camembert and other soft cheeses in the Andersens' household were never, in Beattie's experience, ripe enough to be runny.

But Bob was having considerable trouble confining this expanding, flowing portion of Brie to a solitary biscuit. He tried to transfer some of it onto another but dropped it instead. He then brought the first biscuit at speed to his mouth while attempting to clean up the mess he had made on the low glass-topped table with the pink paper napkin. Beattie found herself forced, despite her great curiosity about the state of the cheese, to shift her gaze to another direction rather than watch him. What was happening was quite bad enough. But she was certain worse was to come. She knew all too well that, completely undaunted by this minor disaster, he would dispose of the biscuit and cheese now in his mouth in no time at all and cut off another large portion of liquified Brie, very likely creating more havoc. A moment later her fears were confirmed. Elizabeth was running towards Bob with a cloth. There was much wiping of table and dabbing at trouser while Bob, head thrown back, was trying not very successfully to look completely *insouciant*. Another glance later showed the table and trousers with damp patches and Bob's plate re-laden.

Beattie took a sip of her drink: a tonic with lemon and ice but no gin. She never took more than one alcoholic drink before dinner. When she had said this, a few minutes before, her hostess had offered her tea.

'I don't suppose you ever drink anything else, do you,

Beattie? I think I've got some someplace at the back of a shelf. We never drink it ourselves.'

'Actually I don't drink it much either. Never just before dinner.' Beattie felt afraid her tone had been sharp to the point of acidity. She found a more amiable note to remark, 'In any case I only really like one particular brand. You can't get it up here. Even down in the City it's only available in one or two places.'

'Oh, really? What's the name of the brand?'

Beattie was surprised by this appearance of genuine interest. Perhaps Elizabeth suddenly suspected tea might be 'in'. Or this form of it anyway.

'I shouldn't tell you. I don't want word to get round. O.K., it's Ling's Pekinese. Luckily Robert can't stand it. One tin lasts me months. Just as well, considering the price. Though as it happens I've run out at the moment. That's a hint to my husband.'

'I'll never remember till Monday. Tell me then.'

'Which shops sell it?' Elizabeth asked.

'Zabar's. One or two others.'

When Elizabeth asked Bob if he too wanted a non-alcoholic drink he had laughed in a way that was half ashamed, half complacent and wholly amused.

'I'm afraid I don't subscribe to my wife's excellent rule,' he said. He requested a gin and tonic with ice.

Beattie now found herself once again faced with Elizabeth heading her way, the customary wide, bright smile fixed on her face, resplendent of eye, tooth and cleavage, carrying a plate and a napkin.

'Help yourself to the cheese, Beattie. Have some of the Brie. It's hot.'

'Hot?'

'Sure. I heated it.'

Beattie allowed her expression to reveal some but not all of her sense of astonishment. But she then experienced and spontaneously showed that relief that comes with a sudden enlightenment. The runniness was fully explained. She accepted the napkin and plate.

'Was that your own idea or did you hear of it some-where?'

'Oh, heavens, it wasn't my own idea, no. Everyone's doing it.'

'Heating their cheese?'

'Right.'

'I wonder how that got started.'

'It's the in thing right now.'

'I must be so out of touch.'

'Try some,' said Bob, indistinctly. 'It's really quite nice.'

Beattie marvelled, as on so many previous occasions, at his absence of shame. Yet she was aware that his habitual gusto was heightened this evening. There was anxiety under it. He had already, despite the difficulties he had earlier got himself into, reduced the hunk of hot Brie by a half and significantly depleted a row of the biscuits.

'Are you having some, Dick?' Elizabeth was holding a plate and a pink paper napkin out to her husband with an air that suggested that whether he wanted them was a matter of no possible interest to her or to anyone. She did not look at them or at him but into the fireplace. All the verve had dropped out of her voice as she asked him the question.

Dick came to life. Beattie thought of the statue in *Don Giovanni* when invited to dinner. But Dick, with two abrupt neck motions, shook his head to mean 'no'. He then shifted position, turning away from the proferred pink napkin, moving his weight onto one leg and unfolding his arms. He looked up and fixed Bob with an intense, anxious stare.

'I have to make an apology.' He twisted his neck a few inches, chin high, easing a crick. 'There's been one helluva goof-up this evening.'

His voice was deep, slow and rasping. When she had first heard it ten months ago Beattie thought he was doing a take-off of an old-style film star. The tone was perfectly matched by Dick's conversational manner, full of that slight-ly uneasy solemnity characteristic of American males in the public arena: actors, generals, men of God, politicians. It was meant to be gracious but was quite without charm. Later, when Dick persisted in talking like that, Beattie realised, with some consternation, that this was no comic parody but his everyday speech.

Dick made a fist of his hand and banged his hip fairly hard. He said, 'It's a bitch. There's not a God-damn thing I can do about it.'

'What's happened?' Bob asked, still with his mouth full, brushing his palms together to rid them of crumbs.

'My partner's coming over later this evening for a business discussion. Liz didn't tell me you were coming to dinner till an hour ago when I walked through the door.'

Beattie felt a sensation of horror fill her whole body. It seemed almost as corporeal a feeling as physical anguish. As it faded she wondered at experiencing so violent a reaction. But it left a sense of dread in its wake, the same dread as she had felt earlier. The suspicions she had had then, on the patio, seemed confirmed. Elizabeth could not have walked up to the house to ask them to dinner. Had she intended to do so she would have discussed it with Dick before he left home. Despite what she said Elizabeth never acted on whim. Sometimes she failed to do what she meant to. But Beattie had never before known her make last-minute plans.

Elizabeth stood, still holding the plate and the pink paper napkin she had unsuccessfully tried to give to her husband, gazing towards him. Her face showed no expression at all. The tanned skin was the colour and smoothness of the polished wood of the panelling lining two sides of the room; the blue eyes were as bland and unvaried as the New England sky curving over them daily. The effect was of some sort of mask: an Aztec one, maybe, though with incongruously Scandinavian features. Beattie had observed to herself on an earlier occasion, and later mentioned to Bob, that Elizabeth's face in repose could have been reproduced as a picture in some questionable but best-selling historical work as evidence that Norsemen discovered the Americas even longer ago than anyone had ever imagined as well as long before anyone else.

Dick fixed his wide, pale blue gaze on Bob's narrower one. (The ogling had, at least for the moment, abated.)

'I have to speak to him, there's no way I can avoid it.'

Bob nodded, his expression showing considerable surprise but his mouth now, after another helping of cheese, too full to speak. Dick transferred the eye contact to Beattie with one continuous move of the head as though it consisted of some invisible liquid he must at no costs let spill.

'It really upsets me to have to leave you while I have a talk with my partner but at this point in time I can't see an alternate course.' He drew himself up very straight and pulled back his shoulders as though to ease still suffering neck musles. He then stretched his arms out behind him. They pointed diagonally off to the sides, giving the overwhelming impression that he was about to take off and fly. But he then brought them forward and folded them over his chest. 'I truly regret this.'

Elizabeth had gone back to the cheeseboard and was busying herself cutting the cheese, facing away.

'It's not something Liz normally does. She's usually preparing days in advance.'

They all stared at Elizabeth's smooth hair and sleek, rounded back. In a moment Elizabeth turned round, her wide smile firmly in place.

'As I told Beattie, it was one of those whims.' She caught each eye in succession and turned back to the cheese.

Dick shook his head. 'I don't even know when he's getting here. I can't call him, he's coming from another appointment. As I said, it's a helluva goof-up.'

Bob said, 'Don't worry. We quite understand.'

Beattie was gazing again at Elizabeth's back. She seemed to Beattie more alien than anyone, male or female, she had met in her life.

'I'll be glad to meet Wayne,' Bob said encouragingly. 'You've told us so much about him.'

'He's a great guy. He's been a Godsend helping me build up the practice. No way could I have done it without him.

With my bit of capital and his experience we've been able to make a real good go of it. I'm expecting great things.'

'Is it some new project you'll be discussing tonight?'

'Wayne's considering buying old Miss Turnhill's property over on Maple. He's getting into the property development line a bit now.'

'I didn't know she was selling.'

'She can't keep the place up any more. She's nearly ninety. She's still very spry, it's amazing, but she can't do as much as she did and her memory's failing her.' He hesitated again, pulling his shoulders back. Then he went on, 'I'm thinking of going in on the purchase. That's what Wayne and I plan to discuss. I happen to be interested in making an investment right now.'

'Oh, really?'

Bob's interest was suddenly sharp, Beattie saw. She wondered briefly whether he thought there was something in this for him. She knew he had visions of moving the business up to New Dartmouth. But she also knew that he was almost incapable of hearing of anyone's plans to do anything without considering whether he ought to participate. She was looking again at Elizabeth. Was there something of hers that Elizabeth wanted that couldn't be purchased? She heard Bob say, 'Would you have any objection to my joining you in discussing this with your partner? I have an interest in the property market myself. Of course, if you'd prefer the meeting to be kept confidential . . .'

'I'd be very happy for you to join our discussion. We'll have to leave the ladies to themselves for a while.'

Beattie saw Elizabeth's back stiffen up slightly. She herself felt a strong surge of resentment and, to her surprise, a strengthening of the dread. At the same time she noted remotely, as though watching somebody else, that her physical being had gone very still. She thought of saying she would go home. She would claim she felt tired or ill. But the prospect of dealing with the ensuing questions and comments and protestations appalled her. She tried catching

Bob's eye but he and Dick were staring into each other's orbs as though they had fallen in love.

'Then again,' Dick went on, 'the price may be too high. Property values are going up real fast around here and old Miss Turnhill's no pushover. In fact, she's quite a shrewd cookie.'

'Sure.' Bob stared into his drink, which he was holding with both hands on his thigh. 'They may have gone up too fast. The boom's flattening out now. Did you know there've been a whole slew of new homes built the builders are stuck with, the demand's fallen off so.'

'Yes, I've heard that.'

'It could be that you might find some investment other than property that might suit you better.'

'Perhaps you're right,' Dick sounded alarmed. His normally perplexed look had intensified to one of real worry.

Elizabeth turned round from the cheeseboard.

'Beattie, won't you have some hot Brie now? Though I'm afraid it's cooled down a little. Let me help you.' Elizabeth picked up a plate. She used the phrase 'help you' in the American sense of 'wait on you'.

Beattie shook her head to mean 'no'.

'Well, *I'm* sure having some.' Elizabeth finished putting some of it on a plate and crossed back over the floorspace in Beattie's direction. 'If you change your mind, Beattie, there's enough here for two.' She sat on the sofa, at the far end from Beattie, and began smearing a knifeful of Brie on a round, bite-sized biscuit.

'I see your hands are still scratched.'

Elizabeth glanced quickly at Beattie, then at her palms.

'A little.'

She turned her long, big-boned hands so they were facing away. Clenching the knife rather tight she resumed smearing her biscuit.

'I don't know what came over Elizabeth.' Dick half turned from Bob to stare at his wife. 'Walking all that way to your house and inviting you to dinner tonight without even asking me whether I had any plans.'

36

Elizabeth put the knife down on the plate. She turned to face Beattie. Her face showed she was about to address her in her most fervent tones.

'Wouldn't you just hate to have to sell your home, Beattie? Like Miss Turnhill's having to?'

'Sure.'

'Poor old lady,' said Bob. 'It's too bad.'

'I wonder where she's moving to?' Beattie said.

Beattie had become quite a close friend of Miss Turnhill. She had visited her in her house three or four times during the year she had lived here. She enjoyed hearing her describe her ancestors' arrival in Massachusetts from Oxfordshire and, a generation later, their move to Connecticut to hew down the forest and plant the first orchards and farms. All those forebears were buried together in a graveyard up on a hill on the Turnhills' vast property.

Despite Beattie's coaxing and hints Miss Turnhill never told one part of her ancestors' story: that of their stealing the land from the Indians. That was a matter, even after two hundred years, that could not be spoken of.

Elizabeth's gaze at Beattie did not waver.

'I'd sure hate to have to sell ours.'

'D'you ever think of selling?' Bob asked Dick. 'With prices so high now?'

'No way. Nothing on earth could induce me to part with this property. There's five years of blood, sweat and tears in this house.'

Elizabeth, ignoring him and still gazing at Beattie, said with unflagging fervour, 'Wouldn't you hate to have to move away from this neighbourhood? Is there anywhere in the whole world as beautiful as the New Dartmouth region? There can't be, I won't believe it if you tell me there is. It just isn't possible.' She inserted the biscuit she was holding while her mouth was still open and clamped her jaws on it firmly. Beattie heard herself say, though she did not really know why, 'I've been to one or two places I think I'd say were as beautiful.'

'India,' said Dick, unexpectedly.

'Have you been to India, Dick?' Bob asked.

'No, but I've heard it's real pretty.'

'I'd like to go to the Himalayas,' said Beattie, though the thought had never previously occurred to her. 'To the top of the world.'

Elizabeth swallowed. 'But not for long, would you, Beattie? Don't you think of this as your home now? Don't you just *love* it?'

'Yeah, sure I love it.'

'With your house so cleverly made into a fabulous residence out of those barns?' Was there the tiniest touch here of conscious hostility? Elizabeth paused for a moment, her eyes still fixed on Beattie's. 'I've never seen a house so adorable. With all the gorgeous old furniture and the pictures and those divine, kooky birds' nests set out in the hall and your fabulous garden? Don't you feel you wanna stay there for ever and ever? That nothing in heaven and earth could make you move anywhere else?' Elizabeth's gaze did not waver throughout this barrage of what Beattie assumed were meant as wholly rhetorical questions. She did not seem for a moment to expect any reaction from Beattie but perfect agreement.

Elizabeth could not see her, Beattie O'Connor, at all. So Beattie found herself thinking.

She must, of course, see a physical being: a body and head; a female-shaped form. And she no doubt observed the white blouse and straight blue skirt and the dark hair piled up in a bun. Although she did not seem generally very observant she had commented on Beattie's blouse when she had first seen her that evening on opening the door. And Elizabeth no doubt observed that Beattie's appearance, or so Beattie hoped and believed and so most people seemed to agree, was attractive and stylish. She gave evidence sometimes of having what Beattie would count as some visual awareness and taste. She had remarked once or twice in what seemed a sensible fashion on pictures and objects. After all, she owned and ran a photographers' gallery. And though her own clothes were not often brilliantly chosen they were never grotesque.

She may perhaps have perceived that appearance to some extent as a challenge or threat. But if so she never made that apparent. She always gave the impression of thinking herself, as a sexual specimen and indeed in all other ways that she considered of consequence, completely un-rivalled.

But, in any case, Beattie felt sure, Elizabeth could not perceive the living, feeling person, with a unique mind and emotions and attitudes and thirty-eight years of life behind her, who was Beattie O'Connor. It seemed not just that Elizabeth lacked intuition and insight; she lacked compre-hension of another being's individual existence. She could not absorb into her understanding of the world about her other people's essential humanity.

Beattie did not reply. She had well noted that Elizabeth had observed the birds' nests arranged on a bench in the hall. She must have done so that morning. She must have been in the house. They would not have been there when she last visited. They had been out at the back under the porch until yesterday.

Beattie had collected the old, empty nests, abandoned the previous year after fulfilling their functions as labour wards, cradles and nurseries to young feathered life early that spring. She had done so in order that the previous occupants would be forced to make new homes for their next batch of eggs. Beattie knew that birds' dwellings are not year round homes: they are constructed solely for breed-ing and raising the next generation. The birds would rear healthier offspring, Beattie believed, in clean, new nests than in re-discovered, re-occupied old ones, all too often falling apart and infested with lice.

Despite their frequently ruinous state Beattie was very fond of the nests. She repaired and restored them, re-weaving loose strands, disinfecting, de-lousing. She liked their rough, woody texture and neat, clever craftsmanship. They pleased her in her capacities both as a creator herself of what she hoped were useful and beautiful objects and as a lover of birds and all creatures. She imagined with pleasure the birds busying themselves with making new homes for the eggs that were coming.

She had meant for the last couple of months to move her collection in from the back porch to the hall and set it out to display it. But she had only the day before at last done so.

Elizabeth kept gazing at Beattie but, getting no sort of response, started to blink rather rapidly. At last she shifted her eyes. They moved to the empty plate Beattie still held on her lap.

'You *must* have some cheese.' She leant over, took Beattie's plate and slid onto it from her own plate her remaining large piece of Brie and a couple of biscuits.

She stood up, holding her plate, and made again for the cheeseboard. Even in the flattering blue dress her pear shape was less well disguised from behind than in front.

Dick said something. Beattie looked round at him. He was again at the room's centre, still on his feet. His hands were clasped behind his raw-looking neck with his elbows stuck out at right angles. He was gazing at her with an expression of *gravitas*. He continued, 'I've only lived in one place before that seemed like home. That was the house I was raised in.'

Beattie opened her mouth to reply but Elizabeth forestalled her.

'I've lived in a dozen places.'

She was facing into the room, standing next to the glass-topped table holding the plate, for once making no eye contact whatsoever with anyone.

'We were in the mid-West when I was small and then California for a while and then we came East.' Her voice was without much expression as though she was not really describing her own life at all. She might have for some reason been couching her remarks in the first person as an author's technique. But there could be detected a faint downbeat note beneath the detachment. It was that sound, often caught on the flip side of the controlled, unemotional tone of a personal narrative, that hints at conflict and misery, even despair, hidden away from the speaker herself. Beattie could not remember Elizabeth ever before displaying so much of her real inner being. She had for some reason forgotten for a moment or two to give a performance.

But then she glanced round at her listeners and her tone changed. It became tinged with false feeling.

'Home was wherever my mother and father and brother were. And then after Dad died just my mother and brother. That's what it is, isn't it, really, a home? It's with the people you love.' She gazed, smiling, from Beattie to Bob. She seemed to have forgotten Dick stood in the room. Or perhaps indeed that he even existed. 'My home's been up here now in Uttoxeter County longer than anywhere else, though.' She still did not acknowledge Dick's presence, let alone the part he had presumably played, judging by what she had said just a moment before, in her feeling that Uttoxeter County was home. 'I've been here since I was twenty. I guess that's one of the reasons I feel like I do about this fabulous, heavenly region.'

Bob, with Elizabeth standing at very close quarters, was staring at her in a way that seemed part ogling, part pretended polite interest, part amazed and amused fascination. Elizabeth glanced down at him, moved a step back and switched on her biggest, most glittering, most vacant smile. Her voice and manner changed from the mildly sentimental to the not at all mildly patronising.

'D'you feel this is your home now, Bob? Up here? Or is your heart still down in the City?'

Bob laughed. 'It's sure not in the City. I hope I never have to live there again.' He put down his glass, with an air of importance. Beattie realised that he was no longer sober. 'For me there's just one ingredient that makes a real home.'

Oh, God, she thought, his tone's aggressive and maudlin. He's gone all Irish. He'll probably start going on about children.

'It's a child. A home's where you raise children.'

41

Dick opened his mouth to reply but Bob went on before he could do so. 'In our case, of course, a child rather than children, alas, though of course we're very grateful for Melly, we're lucky to have her, I never forget that.'

Good God, what's he going to get into, Beattie wondered. He looked abandoned. His hair was chaotic. Is he going to talk about insisting on trying every night, sometimes two or three times, during two-thirds of the cycle for three or four years? Is he going to get into his blaming himself and wondering if he ought to go and have tests and then deciding he shouldn't, it's somehow ungodly? He might even start on theology.

'Of course, we're crazy about Melly, *crazy*. But we wanted a *brood*. I was the eldest of six and I've always had children around me. Beattie was an only child and she didn't want that for Melly. We both wanted more children. But it just hasn't happened.'

Dick shook his head energetically.

'We haven't got kids. But this is our home. You can't put this much effort into designing and building a property and feel as though it's just a roof over your head.

'Yes, this is our home.' Elizabeth's voice startled them all with its tone of extraordinary, saccharine piety.

There was quite a lengthy silence. Everyone stared at her. She was poised on the edge of her seat, half-turned in Beattie's direction. Her eyes looked wider and a deeper blue than ever and perfectly blank. Her face as a whole, insofar as it revealed any expression at all, showed what seemed complacence.

'Dick designed and built this house all himself and it's our home now for ever.'

Bob, Beattie and Dick kept on staring. Then Dick shifted slightly and gave a small cough. 'You helped me, Elizabeth,' he muttered, rubbing his neck. He did not look at his wife. It was hard to be sure whether the inner discomfort expressed on his face was purely embarrassment or if there was some other ingredient present as well. Elizabeth gave no sign whatsoever of having heard what he said. She met Beattie's eye and gave her large-toothed, meaningless smile. Beattie suddenly realised, and at once wondered why she had not done so earlier, that she was not wholly sane.

Chapter
Five

*T*HE gap at one end of the dining-room drapes showed pitch darkness outside. Elizabeth had opened the windows and drawn the heavy green curtains a fraction to let in some air. When everyone was talking or listening Beattie held up her watch to the level of the top of the table to catch its face in the candlelight. It said still not quite half nine. It seemed the middle of night.

The early, rapid coming of darkness in summer as in winter still seemed unusual to Beattie. She missed the lingering evenings she had thought as a child were an essential part of summertime everywhere. There seemed something saddening about the quick-coming night.

Bob was diagonally across the table, beyond a candelabra and various serving dishes at last come to rest, still steaming slightly, after prolonged circulation. His wildness and redness were increased by the candlelight. The dim flickering in this room of heavy formality gave him the look of an erstwhile hard-drinking squire or farmer in some Irish county. But he had sobered up since dinner had started.

He had not spoken now for a while. Beattie had never known him when in company so absorbed in his thoughts. Before dinner he had become if anything even more boisterous than usual. Now he was noticeably quieter. She suddenly wondered if he had sobered up on purpose. It was almost unknown for him to drink his wine slowly. Perhaps he was preparing himself for the meeting with Dick and his partner. This was so very unlike him as to suggest that he really must have some significant interest in taking part in it.

'Didn't you just *love* that movie?'

Beattie realised Elizabeth was talking to her. She looked round and blinked rapidly and summoned her thoughts.

'It all looked a little too glossy I thought. Designer Depression.'

'D'you really think that? I thought it looked *wonderful*.'

She has the same cold, glossy look as the film, it occurred to her. This room has it too.

'Designer Depression,' echoed Dick in appreciative tones. 'That's a pretty good way of putting it.' He twisted his neck sideways and up as if to ease the tension caused by his surprise at this neatly turned phrase.

Bob started giving his views on the movie and Beattie's thoughts again wandered. She glanced at Elizabeth's well-structured profile, showing much tooth and eye in the standard zestful expression. She wondered whether she at heart cared for anyone. She remembered an evening in a bar in the City, on the second storey of a huge plate-glass building, watching small figures across the wide street pouring forth in a blaze of light from the Centre where they had watched Shakespeare or listened to Bach. They were all dressed in dark suits and long dresses and stoles and were all neatly coiffed. Beattie had wondered at their formality. She had not thought of that evening for years. The combination of the conversation and Elizabeth's profile had brought it to mind.

She looked away from Elizabeth and glanced round the room.

A man's figure had appeared silently without any warning in the near darkness by the dining-room door. There was a greater darkness behind him: he must have felt his way down the corridor. He saw that Beattie had seen him. He grinned amiably. He came forward, his short, square form growing clearer as he entered the range of the candlelight.

Bob now saw him as well. He looks a tougher nut altogether than Dick, he thought. He looks a man to be wary of despite the folksy expression.

'Gee, Mrs Andersen, I'd no idea you were having company. I'm sure sorry to disturb you. Dick should have told me not to come till tomorrow.' He had a little-boy voice, deepened a little in pitch from a boy's but quick and ingratiating.

Dick shot round in his seat and hastily and noisily scraped back his chair.

'Wayne, I didn't know you were there. You crept in real quietly.'

He crossed to his partner, clamped his hand onto his and shook it with vigour.

'Come and sit down with us for a minute or two before you and me and Bob here go off to talk privately.' He propelled him, hand now on Wayne's broad, solid back, the short distance across to a free chair at the table.

There was more scraping of chair legs as Bob leapt to his feet, throwing his napkin down on his side plate.

As Wayne came further into the candlelight his face could be seen to be square, the flesh strangely soft-looking.

Dick gripped the back of the spare chair next to Elizabeth's, raising its hind legs by an inch or two. 'Sit here, Wayne. I'm afraid there was a bit of a mix-up this evening.' He explained it, at length, still holding the chair. Elizabeth stood quite still, holding a serving spoon across her chest with her elbow propped up on her left hand, and kept smiling.

Wayne, listening, also stayed on his feet.

'If you're in a hurry we can go straight through now,' Dick said.

'I'm in no hurry.' Wayne came to the table. Dick put the chair legs back down on the floor. Wayne sat down and Dick, it seemed reluctantly, let go of the chair.

Wayne went on, 'But please keep on eating, you folks. You mustn't let that wonderful food that I'm sure Liz has taken so much trouble over go cold.'

'Let me get you some, Wayne. There's ample. I cooked far more than I need. You're starving, I bet.'

'No, I'm fine. I'll just sit here if I may while you finish.'

'You must have a glass of wine, Wayne,' Dick said.

'I thank you. I'd like that.'

'I'm going to give you some dinner whatever you say,' said Elizabeth. 'I won't take no for an answer. You can't have eaten I know.'

'You're a very hard lady to argue with when you want your own way.'

'If you don't eat it it'll just get thrown out.'

'Well, it sure smells delicious.'

'I'll go get a plate.'

Wayne sat now smiling round at them all with an air, Bob thought, of something a touch more than ordinary ease. It was as though he believed he had some special right to have taken his place in their midst at the table.

Bob had observed with great interest the looks that passed between him and Elizabeth. Wayne had kept smiling at her, showing neat, gleaming teeth. He seemed an admirer. Was he more? Elizabeth had received his admiration with what seemed to be mild gratification. Though it was as hard as always to distinguish any real enthusiasm from all the fake zest. In any case, of course, an air of gratification proved nothing.

Bob decided it was very unlikely that they were actually lovers. There would have been more sense of awkwardness between them. Were they heading that way? That was possible. He felt a twinge of what he knew, with a sense of some shame, to be jealousy. This was absurd. Elizabeth had stirred him sexually this evening but the feelings involved were utterly trivial. They could hardly be called feelings at all. They were no more than the workings of glands and secretions. His jealousy was no more a genuine emotion than his mild desire. It was as much a mere reflex. It was sheer male pride.

Bob felt cast in the role of supplanted old lion. Though as it happened an old lion supplanted by one even older. Wayne looked about fifty. But an attractive fifty despite the light voice and soft face. Shrewd; competent; well in control. He looked like a man who, if he wanted to have an affair with Elizabeth Andersen or anyone else, no doubt would. Altogether an unsettling rival, in love or in business.

Bob looked up at Elizabeth as she came back into the room with a plate and a glass and some cutlery. She smiled at him; then at Wayne. Did she make an attempt to seduce every man she encountered? Was it some sort of neurotic compulsion? Had her interest in him been no more than a reflex?

'Here you are, Wayne, it's all cooled down a little by now but it should still be O.K.'

He watched her piling food on Wayne's plate. He felt a regret that he knew even as he was feeling it was not for an opportunity missed or the death of her interest but for all the people and things and events that might have been in his life but now never would.

He felt the familiar quick surge of fear. All the riches he hoped were to come might be lost. He picked up his knife and fork and quickly cut into the remains of his now cooling fish. He pushed the fear down, out of mind.

Soon after, Dick proposed that the three men go to his den.

Chapter
Six

ELIZABETH was clearing the table. She seemed strangely
preoccupied. Beattie watched her put a large plate on
top of a small one, add some glasses and knives and discover
on lifting the whole that her fingers could scarcely reach
round to the bottom. She hurriedly put the unstable con-
struction back down. Beattie rose from her seat and, in a
token gesture of helping, moved slowly the length of the
table, gathering together the greasy, crumpled pink paper
napkins and squeezing them into a ball in her hands.
She dropped it into a dish. She stretched up, pulling her
shoulders back, wondering what more, if anything, by way
of appearing to help, to embark on.

Elizabeth had started again. After a while she put the
last plate on the new pile she had constructed and said,

'D'you wanna go for a swim in the pool?' She did not look Beattie's way.

There was a pause. Beattie considered the unexpected but not all that surprising proposal. People with pools often suggested a swim, morning, evening or night-time. Yet it passed through her mind that there might be something to this suggestion beyond a lap or two under the stars. But this seemed unlikely. She could not imagine Elizabeth Andersen hosting an orgy. And what else could she mean?

Beattie sat down again, on the chair that was nearest, still wondering what she should do. Elizabeth had begun gathering up cutlery. She glanced round, caught Beattie's eye and smiled a moderate version of the wide smile and revved up her manner to something approaching its customary cold zest.

'It'd cool you right down. It's a hot night. They'll be an hour at least in there talking.' She held Beattie's gaze for a moment, then, looking away, leaned against the table, her hands full of forks. 'Once Dick and Wayne get onto business there's nothing'll stop them. I expect Bob's the same.'

'Aren't all men? Talking business makes them feel they're important.'

'Right.'

Elizabeth transferred the forks to her left hand and picked up a serving spoon with her right.

'I don't think you've ever been in our pool, have you, Beattie?'

'Once.'

Elizabeth had often invited her to bring Melly round for a swim; Beattie had after the first time not accepted these offers.

'You really should try it again.' Elizabeth pushed herself upright and began moving, shifting the spoon into the hand with the forks in it, glancing over the table.

It *was* a hot night. That is, it was hot in the house; Beattie guessed it was considerably cooler outside. The strong sense that at once filled her mind of the coolness and darkness and scented air and soft forest noises made her push back her chair and glance at the door.

'I often go for a dip after dinner,' Elizabeth said, now reaching for glasses.

'Isn't it a bit too soon after dinner right now?'

'I know people say not to swim after a meal but I've never found it a problem. As you know, Beattie, I don't cook heavy meals.' She stood still a moment, holding two glasses in one hand, two fingers in each. Certainly the meal Beattie had eaten had not been at all heavy. She had left a lot of each course on her plate. The sea bass had been overcooked, the rice sticky, the vegetables raw. The dessert had been a large, sticky cake, laden with sweetened whipped cream, glacé fruits and chopped walnuts nearing the end of their lifespan.

Beattie stood up. She had decided. A swim *would* be nice. She could do lots of slow laps through the cool water and need speak not a word to Elizabeth Andersen.

'We've got a great diving board. Bob didn't want to get it because of the extra expense but I made him. I adore diving. It's real high, you get a good plunge. You're terrific at swimming and diving I know. I've seen you, down at the beach.'

'I always go in with a dive.'

'It looks so stylish, when someone goes right in like that off a board. D'you wanna wear one of my suits?'

Beattie did *not* want to wear one of Elizabeth Andersen's suits. The thought of it pressed to her skin, in her most intimate places, revolted her. She asked herself if she minded swimming unsuited. People often did so in this land, under cover of darkness. 'Skinny dipping' was an activity of licensed sexual daring in this primmest of nations. She decided that in any case no one was likely to see her, not even, if she could possibly help it, Elizabeth Andersen. She would stay well under water while Elizabeth was anywhere near.

'I'll swim nude.'

'Sure. Why not? I often do though I guess I'll wear a swimsuit this evening.' She paused, as though about to offer a reason. Perhaps she was trying to think of one. If so she failed. It struck Beattie that her claim often to swim in the nude might be pure invention, produced of the wish to seem bold.

She went on, 'You go on ahead. Take off your clothes in the cabana. It's right near the diving board. I'll go get my suit and a couple of towels and join you as soon as I can. I'll switch the pool lights on as I come out through the hallway.'

The night was dark but not pitch. The air was cooler than inside the house. However, it was warm enough still to make the prospect of a swim seem enticing. There was a sliver of moon in the sky and a great many stars.

A pool of faint light cast from a window, whose drapes were not drawn all the way, lay on the ground. It silvered the gravel and, a few feet further off, beyond the edge of the path, purpled the grass till it faded to blackness. By day this land could be seen as a clearing hewn only recently. A few tree-stumps remained here and there in the roughly mown grass. One or two logs lay around, sawn ends pale. Some way away near the edge of the forest was what seemed a piece of the sky overhead condensed into water.

But now liquid was black as hard ground.

However, near where the pool lay unseen was a form in the darkness, of still deeper blackness, which Beattie knew from its shape and dimensions must be the structure supporting the diving board. She took off her shoes and, carrying them, set off towards it, stepping slowly and carefully. There might be prickles and thorns in the grass. But she felt nothing worse underfoot then the pitted and uneven ground and the rough verdure and an occasional small stone. The structure transformed itself gradually, as she came close to it, from a shadowy shape into posts and a ladder. Nearby, a few yards away to the left, was a smaller shape which she knew must be the hut that Elizabeth had called the cabana.

It was too dark in there to see anything. She felt round for a chair or a shelf – a surface of any kind – and found some rough, level wood at just above knee height. She put her shoes on it: then undressed. She folded her clothes and placed them on top of the shoes since the bench, or whatever it was, might be dirty. She unscrewed her earrings and placed them on top of the pile.

She stepped out of the hut and walked through the back towards the shape, fairly clearly discernable at this short distance but again gaining greater solidity as she came closer, of the diving-board ladder.

The air felt cool on her skin. She was very aware of the sensation of movement unhindered by clothes. She had never before gone naked outdoors. The effect was both unnerving and sensuous. She thought: this is how it must be all the time for the animals. My kitten feels this freedom from anything touching its body and restricting its movements. But its fur must feel different from skin. There is no other creature that moves through the night in bare membrane as we do. This sensation of sensuous freedom is unique to mankind. She saw in her mind nearly naked American Indians as shown in old-fashioned geography textbooks for very young children, holding aloft bows and arrows, tan skin glistening. She saw even earlier men, of the Stone Age, bearing over their heads spears poised for throwing. People must have gone naked over the earth for millennia. Surely they must have sometimes been conscious of what she was now feeling. They cannot have taken their nakedness, out in the air and the darkness, always for granted.

Beattie imagined herself as a squaw in this forest a long time ago: a thousand years, perhaps ten thousand. She was free for an hour or two from her man and her children. She was away from her tribe. She was alone and at peace in the darkness and night. As she trod the grass silently she felt a strong sense of belonging here, in this land and this forest, under the sky pricked with stars and the slender, curved moon.

She heard a rustling nearby. She stopped. But she could see nothing on the ground near her feet except unvarying blackness.

She walked on, treading even more carefully. She had remembered that moment last autumn when, walking alone, she had glimpsed inches away a rattlesnake slithering into the grass.

She had stepped off the main thoroughfare that led from the village of New Monmouth to the Lake Tocahoe beach, to walk down a side road, no more than a track. It had descended to the edge of the stream that ran through the village and into the woods. She felt a sense of deep solitude. She felt sure no one normally walked here. Yet this route had in past time for thousands of years been trodden by Indians. She felt she knew this as surely as if she had seen their dim shades come slipping noiselessly out from the trees to walk it beside her.

She heard the rustling again. She stopped. The sound ceased. She walked on towards the enlarging shape of the structure supporting the diving board.

The Indians had walked here, too, over this land that at present belonged to the Andersens; it would then have still been uncleared. The Indian braves would have come to these woods hunting rabbits and deer. They would have searched for berries and nuts and at nightfall lain down to sleep in the hollows of tree-roots. Perhaps they had gazed up at the moon and stars and then curled round, closing their eyes, and dreamed of the creatures they hunted, whose terrain, this dark forest, they shared.

Beattie stopped at the base of the diving-board ladder and looked up at the sky. With an imaginative thrust, a twist of perception and knowing, she discarded the notion that those points and that sliver of light were vast, solid spheres, distant by expanses of space from her planet. She saw them as a part with the earth on which she was standing of an undivided Creation. She felt herself part of that too. This forest and land and all the physical world were, for these moments, her home.

She stood watching and listening. An owl hooted not far off in the forest. A cloud blacked out the moon. There were fewer stars now than there had been. The night was darker.

Even as she continued to gaze a few stars dimmed and failed. It was as dark as it could be.

It occurred to her that Elizabeth was taking her time about switching the lights on. Perhaps she was still upstairs re-applying her make-up. Or re-doing her hair. Or trying on various swimsuits to see which most flattered her figure in case she was seen by the men. But Beattie did not mind the delay.

She stepped onto the diving-board ladder and took hold of the rail. It felt cold to the touch. She began slowly to climb up the steps.

These felt rough under her feet. She moved slowly on upwards. The steps, the rail, the top of the ladder, were invisible now in the blackness. There was for a moment a hint of a breeze: it passed, leaving the air as still as it had been. Beattie was no longer the Indian squaw. But neither was she her quotidian self. She had been altered. The part of her that was her own distinct being was lessened. Everything else had acquired new density.

As she glanced up at the sky and forward into the forest and down to where the pool lay unseen the deep night seemed not just an absence of light but a solid reality. She imagined the liquid below her, silky and still, waiting to swallow her. She wondered if it was cold.

She reached the top of the stairs and stepped onto the diving board. The canvas surface was rougher under her feet than the steps, with a warmer, more prickly feel to it. She walked the length of the board, its spring echoing the lift of her spirits as she had climbed upwards. She knew when she had got to the end by the 'give' of the board. She stood for a moment, poised aloft in the air and the shade. She felt more alone than ever before in her life and yet richly accompanied. She had come into her own.

Beattie pushed down with her weight, bending her knees. She made the board bounce, swinging her arms. Then she lifted her hands high over her head in the diving position. Instead of diving at once she brought her arms back behind her and bounced up and down again a few times. She

57

enjoyed diving: as Elizabeth had said, a few minutes before, she was excellent at it. This moment of readying herself for the plunge was always exhilarating. Now, in the darkness, it was more so than ever. The prospect of diving off into blackness and hitting the water unseen beneath her was thrilling.

She swung her arms forward to bring them up once more in position. As she did so she felt something cool and hard slip over her hand. She realised at once that it must be her bracelet. She had forgotten to take it off when she undressed in the darkness. As her palms met over her head she awaited the splash.

There was a soft, sharp sound, giving rise to an echo so faint and brief as to be almost inaudible. An instant after there was another small sound, even softer, and then another, softer still. She stayed immobile a moment, arms still aloft. Then she brought them down in front of her chest, palms together, fingers entwined. She started shaking all over.

The great space of darkness below her was altered to a vast and invisible cavern of death. The end of life was a footstep away.

For a long while she dared make no movement. Then she began to step slowly, very carefully backwards. Her chest and whole being were full of a furious terror. The whole physical universe seemed now turned against her. The very air was an enemy. Her shaking put her at increased risk of falling but she could not control it. She was torn between a desire to go down on her knees and a fear, in so doing, of losing her footing. She stayed upright. She could not make out the edge of the board in the blackness. She did not dare to try to turn round. Holding one hand behind her ready to meet the high rail at the top of the steps and encountering nothing but air she lost all grasp of the extent of the passage of time. She had been treading that board, facing backwards, for ever. She might continue to tread it till she stepped into whatever new, waiting world exists out in the dark beyond this one.

When her hand touched the cold rail at last she felt for a moment sheer disbelief. It was as though she had already passed into another existence and this tangible evidence of the mundane could be only a dream. But then she understood she was anchored again to this earth. She felt relief pouring through her. She would remain her known self. She would continue to live inside years without pre-recognised limits.

She stretched a foot down behind her, met the top stair, climbed down at high speed, collapsed onto the ground and, still shaking, broke into long, gasping sobs.

Light suddenly filled the night air. Beattie crawled to the edge of the pool and looked down. Her bracelet shone white against grey at the base of the slope on the pool's concrete floor.

She leapt up, ran into the hut and pulled on her clothes and shoes and began to run to the house. Elizabeth was coming towards her, clearly seen in the glare of the lights from the poolside, in a green and yellow striped swimsuit, one towel round her shoulders, holding another. She stopped.

'Beattie!'

There was a look on her face that seemed wondering and alarmed but, Beattie thought, unsurprised.

Beattie did not answer her or slow down but looked away and kept running.

She did not know which door led to the den; she tried several; she suddenly found herself facing three startled men's faces.

'Bob . . .'

'What's the matter?' Bob was coming towards her.

All three men gathered close. Bob put his arm round her shoulders.

'I . . . Oh, Bob . . . the pool . . .'

She let Bob hold her to his chest tightly. She was startled to feel against its hardness and firmness how violently she was still shaking.

'What's happened?'

The only words she could push from her tight, sobbing throat were, 'I want to go home.'

'Beattie . . .'

She tugged at his shirt, like a child.

'But what's *happened*?'

The scene seemed to last for an age, Bob holding his ground, all three men talking at once, Beattie still sobbing and violently shaking, scarcely able to speak, yet aware of herself as fully alert to all that was happening. Elizabeth appeared on the edge of the group.

'D'you know what's happened here?' Dick asked her angrily, as though he assumed immediately she was in some way responsible.

'I've no idea.' Her eyes were very wide, her expression unreadable. 'Beattie suddenly came running right past me back from the pool. I was about to join her there for a swim.'

There was the briefest of pauses.

'A swim!' Dick sounded awed. Husband and wife were staring into one another's wide eyes as though they were scarcely acquainted and surprised by each other's un-expected arrival in this place at this time. Dick said, 'But I drained the pool yesterday to clean it.'

Elizabeth did not immediately answer.

'Didn't you know that, Elizabeth?' Dick leaned a little towards her.

'No.'

'I must have told you.'

'You didn't tell me.'

'My God, Beattie.' Bob clutched his wife to him in both arms as though to crush her into himself. She knew he had grasped at once all that had happened. All the same she said, 'I was on the board. I almost dived . . .'

'Oh, my God.' Bob buried his face in her hair. He kept intoning her name and 'Oh, my God' and once, the words half-dissolved in her hair, 'I could have lost you' or 'I almost lost you'.

'My bracelet slid off.'

60

'Oh, Jesus,' Bob whispered, still into her hair, under-standing it all.

'I heard it hit concrete.'

'Oh, Beattie.'

'I want to go home.'

'Elizabeth, I *told* you I was going to empty the pool. I know I told you.'

'You didn't, Dick. I'd no notion you were even *thinking* of emptying the pool.'

'Please let's go.'

'Why don't you sit down?' Dick's round, pink face, lined with distress, peered into Beattie's, round Bob's bulky chest.

'I want to go.'

'Let me get you a drink. I can't tell you how terrible I feel about this. I just thank God you weren't . . .'

Bob started moving Beattie away to the door, his arm tight round her shoulder.

'I'll ring you tomorrow, Dick.'

'How can I ever . . .' Elizabeth stood, still in her swim-suit, arms akimbo in a gesture meant, it appeared, to express her remorse, her eyes wild. Beattie looked quickly away from her.

Chapter
Seven

*B*OB gently and carefully pulled his arm out from under her. He slid off the sofa and laid her back down on the cushions. Then he bent further over to lift her bare legs and place them so that she lay at full length. After that he raised her dropped arm and replaced it along the length of the now grubby white blouse and ridden-up, wrinkled tight skirt. Really just as though she was dead. My God, she so easily could have been. He felt the warmth of her arm as he held it to be something almost miraculous, something meriting profound, stirring gratitude. She was breathing deeply, with a suggestion of snoring. The two large brandies he had given her had had rapid effect. She had drunk them quickly, still shaking, as she had re-lived, in describing it to him in detail, what she had gone through. Then, warm in his arms, her head on his shoulder, she had fallen asleep.

In the car on the way home she had been sobbing and could say nothing coherent except 'She was trying to kill me.' She had kept repeating the phrase, in a tone of shocked awe at the grandeur and magnitude of what so nearly had happened and, at the same time, of an outrage that seemed somehow childlike. 'How could she?' her tone seemed to imply. 'How could anyone *do* that to me? That's not fair. That's not *meant* to happen.' Bob, glancing sideways at the distraught figure beside him, said two or three times, 'Don't try to talk, wait till we're home.' It occurred to him that at last the fearless Beattie had known fear as others do. Her nervelessness had failed her.

Now he knelt down by the sofa and prayed. He thanked God, several times over, for sparing her life.

He stood up and poured himself a third brandy. (His drinking had kept pace with hers.) Then he sat down in the armchair which stood a few feet from and facing the sofa and considered Beattie's delusion that Elizabeth Andersen had been trying to kill her. It seemed natural enough in the circumstances. Beattie's mind had already been filled with the notion that Elizabeth had had some strange motive when she came to the house. He felt renewed thankfulness that he had never told her about what had occurred between himself and Elizabeth that hot day eight or nine months before. God knows what she would have read into *that*, in the light of what had just happened. On the other hand, if he had told Beattie they would not have been at the Andersens that evening at all. They would never have gone there again. And that of course was why he had not told her. At least . . . Well, yes, that *was* why. Or, anyway, that was the chief, most significant reason.

There had been a faint chlorine smell as well as a whiff of warm dampness. He had been aware of a deep V and that smooth, rounded swelling of stomach, bottom and hips that was the flaw in Elizabeth's figure but now was strangely compelling. The glare of the sunlight made the blueness of her eyes seem paler than usual with a metallic, light shine. He had thrust out his hand, clutching a book: the cause of his visit. She had lifted her hand as though she would take it but then held it suspended. She had remembered, she said, that her hands were still wet from the pool. She had asked him to come into the house and had placed her damp fingers over his wrist as though gently to lead him. He had opened his mouth to reply to her but no sounds had come out. His vocal chords had seemed welded together. She and he had stood for what seemed an age, she gazing into his eyes, he moving his tongue, lips and jaws to no verbal effect. He had felt panic and a sense of absurdity and considerable wonderment.

At last she had removed her hand from his wrist and the power of speech was returned to him.

'I have to get back straightaway.'

'But you *can't*.'

The last word had been almost a wail. Bob had at that point nearly succumbed to that eerily genuine cry of distress, to the tanned flesh and the blueness. But he saw the metallic gleam still. He held himself back.

'Dick's out, he won't be back till this evening. Come for a dip in the pool.'

'No, I really can't stay.'

'Then come indoors for a minute or two just for a coke.' She tossed back the extraordinarily glossy brown hair. It was not wet at all except at the ends.

'I think I'd really better just leave the book. Beattie's expecting me.'

'Do you always do everything Beattie expects?'

'Almost always.'

'The perfect husband, huh, Bob?'

'I try to be.'

'Lucky Beattie.'

'I'm not *that* perfect.'

'Look, if you can't stay now why not come by some other time? Like Monday? Dick's out late on Monday.'

'No.'

'Not interested, Bob?'

'Look, Elizabeth, I'd better be plain, I'm a boringly faithful old husband, I always have been, I'm going to go on being so if I possibly can.'

'You mean you're *never* unfaithful?'

'I don't mean to sound pious. That's how it is. I won't say I'm not tempted sometimes.'

'Like now?'

'Yes, like now.'

'She'd never know.'

'I know it probably sounds kinda strange but the fact is I'm a practising Catholic and I really do believe adultery's a sin.'

Elizabeth turned away. Then she looked back.

'Oh, look, Bob, come in and have a Coke anyway. Just for ten minutes.' She laughed. 'After all, we're neighbours and friends. I'll go put something on.'

'I wouldn't trust myself.'

Elizabeth smiled. She gazed at him a few moments longer, then sighed and looked away over the clearing. He made a movement to go. She stopped him by saying, 'What would you and Beattie do if you didn't get on?'

'Stick it out, I guess. Try to work out the differences.'

'But what if they wouldn't work out?'

'We'd keep trying.'

'For ever?'

'I guess so.'

'What if one of you fell in love with somebody else?'

'Same thing.'

'Is divorce still wrong for you Catholics?'

'It's not wrong, it's impossible.'

'No such thing, huh?'

'That's right.'

'Only death.'

Elizabeth laughed. She turned away, then looked round, smiled, turned again and walked off to the house.

When Bob met her again she behaved as if nothing had happened between them. It seemed hard now to believe that it had. Elizabeth never gave him a sign that her offer might still be open. It must, for her, have been a day's passing fancy.

Beattie stirred a little and sighed. Bob wondered whether she would ever again consent to go to the Andersens. At best relations would be strained for some time. This near disaster had happened at the worst possible moment. He felt the old terror but it was quickly dissolved by a stronger, more secure feeling of hope than he had known for some days. This incident might not have come at a bad time after all. It might serve a purpose.

Bob thought for a while about the meeting with Dick and his partner. Though it had ended so suddenly he had learnt as much as he needed to know: how much Dick had to invest; when his money was needed. He learned that Wayne had abandoned the plan to buy Miss Turnhill's property in favour of waiting till a larger piece of land that he knew of, more potentially profitable after development, came on the market in two or three weeks. Dick had a large sum of money, immediately available, with nowhere special to go for the length of that time. Bob planned to present his case to Dick the next day for lending him what he needed to save him from bankruptcy. Just for one or two weeks. That was as long as he'd need it for. Such a loan would solve the immediate problem and give him time to recoup and make plans for the future. The amount Dick had available admittedly would not quite meet the need. But Bob hoped to persuade him to take out a mortgage as well. Just for one or two weeks. The idea had been forming and now presented itself clear and whole in his mind that Beattie's near death at Dick and Elizabeth's hands, however unplanned, would give him an enormous psychological and moral advantage in requesting the loan.

He would persuade Dick to say nothing to Wayne.

Bob gazed at Beattie's bedraggled, slim figure. Her bun had long since disintegrated and her hair flowed over her shoulders. One of the pearly buttons was undone: the tight skirt had ridden up high, revealing the edge of a pair of frilly white knickers. He felt a stirring of the libido that had lain dormant awhile. He knew suddenly without making a conscious decision that he would say nothing to Beattie of what he was planning. Of course there was no risk to Dick. Of that he felt certain. But Beattie might find this hard to believe. She should have no further worries to cope with till she had got over her shock. He would turn the tide of his fortunes, avoid disaster, put everything right, without her needing to know there had ever been trouble.

He finished his brandy and glanced at his watch. It was half past eleven. It seemed very much later.

Gazing at Beattie's still form he asked himself if he had the physical strength to carry her in his arms up to bed. He had done this once or twice long ago as an amorous gesture. But then he had been many years younger and strengthened by passion. Besides, that had been in the City apartment, which did not have stairs.

Beattie's head made a small, twitching movement; her mouth fell open a fraction; she gave a light snore. Her body turned on the sofa: one leg, left behind, dropped from the knee over the edge. Perhaps she was dreaming. Then she lay still again. The quietness of the night seemed to deepen. There was no creaking, no faint sounds from the forest. Bob glanced round. The huge room, once a storehouse for grain, dimly lit by one lamp, faded to blackness at the far end. Beattie stayed still. There was no movement anywhere. Bob thought, this is tranquillity: but how fragile, how close to its opposite. He gazed again at his wife, dishevelled, a little graceless in the posture into which she had moved but in his eyes still uniquely desirable. He felt he could not awaken her. She would remember at once what had happened: her eyes would widen in horror; she would start up; she might begin again that soul-piercing shaking and sobbing.

Bob went to the sofa, bent down and pushed his arms under her. As he stood up, and at the same time lifted her body, he managed to shift her head so that it leant on his shoulder. She felt lighter than he had anticipated. He remembered carrying his daughter like this a few months before, after a fall in the snow when he and she were outside in the grounds playing snowballs. Beattie was lighter.

The walk across the long room, down the few steps to the hall and then up the flight of stairs to the landing was easier than he had expected. His way was lit by the light in the hall which he had switched on when he and Beattie entered the house. He pushed open the bedroom door with his shoulder. Inside it was dark but, acquainted as he was with the layout, he found the bed easily. He lay Beattie down, switched on the small bedside lamp and sat resting beside her. His arms ached: his body felt heavy: his strength seemed used up.

She had fallen into a spreadeagled posture, her head back and chin high. He wondered if he ought to undress her. It seemed wrong to leave her lying there in her clothes though he did not really know why. There would be no sex tonight, he assumed. Beattie looked as though she would sleep for eight or nine hours. He felt mildly aroused, but exhausted. He could wait until morning.

He pushed Beattie's hair away from her shoulders and neck. The strands felt surprisingly silky. Was her hair always like that and he had failed to observe it? Was that possible? Were there things about people, obvious things, unnoticed by their spouses for twelve or more years? Very likely there were. How separate were even those who were closest. Beattie seemed so apart from himself as she lay there before him. She looked enclosed and unknowable. There had been a time early on when she and he had believed that their souls had been cut from the very same cloth and could be stitched into one. But he knew now each soul was of separate stuff. He had always known that but only in theory. Now he knew it as he knew he breathed air and walked on the earth. He had learned it as a truth of the heart during the passage of time and the course of his marriage. He had come to know Beattie better than anyone else in the world, perhaps as well as he or anyone else could ever know anyone. As a result, by failing still really to know her, he had discovered that discrete, unique essence at the core of each individual. It occurred to him that through a deep knowledge of what was particular he had learned something that was generally true: and so it is always. He touched her cheek with his fingers: he gave a sigh of admiration but also of acceptance of her limits and faults: a sigh of long-married love.

He started undoing her pearly blouse buttons, in the process becoming far more aroused, though not uncontrollably. He thought, I should do this disrobing more often. The words came into his mind: it's a neglected region of marital pleasure. He liked them: he would say them sometime, perhaps in the morning, to Beattie. He pushed her onto her side and slid the blouse down over one arm. What smooth skin she has: I like her like this; she's more totally mine in this state than she ever is when awake. He rolled her the other way, slid the blouse off the other arm and then, using both hands, pulled it out from beneath her. She was wearing a simple white bra: he thought, how girlish it looks. He reached over her with both arms to unhook its clasp at the back. The click and the loosening, the bra's coming away like a mould from the substance within it, increased his excitement. I used to do this when we were young and both full of enjoyment of each part of the process of going to bed and both terribly eager: how long ago it seems now, years and years: it's good I remembered the knack of it; perhaps it's like riding a bicycle, once learned, not forgotten . . . How sweet her breasts look: I wish she'd wake up: perhaps she will, after all: but I mustn't cause it on purpose. He reached down behind her with his right hand to unzip her skirt and then hoisted her up and slid the skirt over her legs. Then he reached for her knickers and slid them off too. Her nakedness reminded him of his fantasy on the drive from the City. It seemed now a strange premonition. Bob quickly took off his clothes, lay down on the bed, switched off the light, took his wife in his arms and began stroking her, restraining his caresses to the gentle and tender though his feelings were passionate.

Beattie sighed and arched her back slightly and shifted her legs so that they came slightly apart and muttered one or

70

two indistinguishable words. She turned her head and spoke Bob's name clearly. Bob, losing control, believing she was awake, climbed on top of her and, as she gave a small moan of seeming assent, pushed her legs further apart with his hand and thrust himself into her.

Beattie's body went rigid. She raised her head.

'Oh, my God . . .' She sounded as utterly terrified as she had when she came back from the pool and had gazed at him, her eyes wide and frantic, scarcely able to speak.

But Bob could not stop now.

'Darling.'

'Oh, my God.'

'I love you, darling, I love you.'

'Bob . . .'

'It's O.K., darling, it's me, Bob . . .'

'My God.'

'Beattie, Beattie.'

She said nothing more. After a while it was over.

'Darling . . .'

'Jesus, Bob.' She no longer seemed frightened: but she was now completely distraught.

'Beattie . . .' Bob tried to caress her. He felt a shaming but almost overpowering desire for sleep. He murmured, 'I thought you wanted me to . . .'

'I didn't know what was happening.' She jerked her arm abruptly away from him.

'Oh, Beattie, I'm sorry, I wanted you so . . .'

'But, *God.*'

'It's all right now, love.'

'That was barbaric.'

Bob felt a sick misery and a strong sense of hurt but at the same time, and shamingly, a continuing almost irresistible longing for sleep.

'Completely barbaric.'

'I didn't know you'd be frightened like that.' He tried again to caress her but again she would not let him. He repeated, mumbling, 'You seemed awake.'

'You could have asked me if I was awake.'

'Of course you've just . . .'

'I've just what?'

'Naturally you're upset in the circumstances.'

'I'd have been upset whatever the circumstances. Does that surprise you?'

His eyes were closing.

'I don't know, Beattie.'

'It's not the slightest surprising.'

He forced his eyes open. He lifted himself on his elbow and gazed towards where she invisibly lay.

'Beattie, darling, don't be angry.'

'It was brutal.'

'What did you think was happening, love? Didn't you know it was me?'

'I don't know what I knew.'

'Did you think I was a rapist?'

'You were a rapist.'

'Oh, God, O.K., I'm sorry.'

She got out of bed; he lay back; his eyes closed; within moments he had lost consciousness.

Her hands were shaking so much she had difficulty turning the taps. Her wrists seemed as though weak with disease. At last hot water cascaded down over her, in that way that it had, coming hard and fast suddenly. She wetted and soaped the sponge and began at once to wash between her legs and over the bony, hair-covered mound above where they parted. She opened her thighs very wide, becoming bow-legged, to make sure she missed no crease or crevice, vigorously squeezing and sloshing the sopping wet sponge against every piece of tight and loose flesh, and then poking it as far as she could up inside her. The near catastrophe, the just missed collision, might be followed by a disaster that was far from a miss. It might be a straight aim and hit at a moving but easy-placed target, a poison-tipped arrow shot directly to the centre of body and life.

She rinsed out the sponge and applied it again with unflagging energy, washing off soap with the semen. Oh,

God, don't let it have happened. Her period had finished a week ago now: it had been over, she could recall, before Bob had gone to the City. She was right slap bang in the midst of her menstrual cycle. She could not bear to go through it again: the pain and indignity; the humiliation; the patronage of those white-coated people in charge. They had gathered round, smiling condescendingly, talking to and about her in a facetious, almost giggling manner, as though she were an idiot. She lay, naked except for that surgical sackcloth, in direst pain. And then there was the ugliness afterwards, the child gone from her womb but her flesh still swollen and wrinkled and slack; the crying and smells; the pain in her nipples and womb; the aching, endless exhaustion. She would never ever go through that again.

Bob had said he wanted a brood. She was not able to tell him she would bear him no more after this one. It could provoke a crisis that would shatter their marriage.

His desire for more children was, she had told herself, based on illusion. It was a part of that detritus of American Irish Catholicism that, in some moods, she viewed with benevolent tolerance but, in others, despised. At the start of their marriage the former mood had predominated. But now she at times felt something close to despair that the fall-out from his religious and national heritage made up so much of his thinking and feeling. She never overtly took issue with it. She felt powerless to do so without angering him and causing conflict between them. She had never in her life, by intention, caused conflict. He might guess at some of her feelings but she never overtly expressed them.

At times her impatience extended to his core of belief. She felt sure that his faith in an afterlife derived from his egotistical terror of ceasing to be. She sometimes wanted to flee from that egotism. Her love had so far withstood that desire but she was not wholly certain it would do so for ever.

Meanwhile, she felt unable to regard his desire for more children as deep or significant. She believed it to be of a piece with his solemnity about observing St Patrick's Day and the possibility, sometime, of taking a second trip to, or even living for a while in, the land of his ancestors. This feeling for 'roots', in him or in anyone, was, she was convinced, intrinsically false. His mental picture of and beliefs about the country that his great-grandparents had come from corresponded hardly at all to the current reality.

And, in time, he would learn for himself that one child was enough to absorb all the love one could give.

At moments she was overwhelmed by a sense of terrified guilt at what she was doing. Her own action seemed when she properly thought of it scarcely believable. It seemed surely not possible that she had for ten years been deceiving the husband whom, despite all the differences between them, she loved.

But her horror at the thought of ever becoming pregnant again made her go on deceiving him.

There was however no further recourse now that this appalling risk had been taken. She washed the rest of her body, stepped out of the shower and dried herself. She sprinkled talc over her arms and stomach and breasts. The amateur douche, she knew, must have been futile. An insertion of spermicide would be equally pointless.

However, Bob might want to make love again.

She took the small blue plastic spongebag, adorned with pink flowers, its top gathered neatly together with ribbon, from where it was hidden behind soap and toilet rolls under the sink. This bathroom was her own and Bob never came into it. There was of course always the risk that for some unlikely reason – to do, maybe, with fire or flood – he would have a reason to enter and would find and look into the spongebag. But he never had, for ten years. And Beattie could live with a risk. Perhaps, as Bob surmised, she in some obscure way liked to.

He had never felt anything inside her that made him suspect. She had been sure he would not. She had used the device with other men, before marriage. Her strong impression had always been that they could not tell it was there.

74

She took out the round, brown rubber diaphragm, smeared it with cream, and, squatting, pressed the sides close together and pushed it up into her.

Chapter Eight

ELIZABETH felt the customary sense of unease as she stepped into the elevator. It was empty apart from herself. She wished hard that someone – anyone – would appear through the door from the street and follow her in. But as she turned to face outwards the doors softly closed.

That wait before anything happened seemed as always to last for longer than normal. As always Elizabeth decided that this stupid, out-dated contraption, due for replacement long since, must have stopped working. As always she wanted to scream. As always the elevator shook very slightly as it started, incredibly slowly, to move. As always she felt momentary relief.

However, once the shaking had passed there was no longer any sensation of movement at all. Elizabeth watched for the third in the series of numbers over the doors – the 2 – to light up. (The 2 came above B for basement and 1 for first floor.) Then she would know for a certainty the lift was in motion. She again felt relief as what she was anxiously waiting for happened. But as the elevator continued on upwards, the floor numbers one by one lighting and fading, the unease again became stronger. Elizabeth took several slow breaths. The elevator might stop between floors; the doors might remain closed when it reached the top floor; the lift might begin to descend, falling faster and faster, at last crashing into the earth to bury her deep, perhaps at first still alive.

She felt that ghostly sensation of terror which is both foreboding and filtered remembrance.

She had known and endured the fear that her mind now gave shadowy form to. That it was only partly remembered and not fully imaginable made it all the more horrible. It had been judged by the mysterious interior censor too fearful for conscious awareness. It had split and was still splitting the mind from itself.

The suffering was there, undiminished though hidden. The main events and a fraction of the emotion were in an outermost chamber, always available; some of the details and much of the feeling were in a room with a door normally closed; the full horror was in a place locked and bolted. Yet it could not be kept entirely and always incarcerated: it could like a witch alter forms: it could shrink to something invisible: it could liquify; vapourise: it could emerge surreptitiously.

Elizabeth's palms were wet. Her heart was beating fast. She looked all round and above her, seeking distraction. There was her face at an angle between a wall and the ceiling, cheeks broadened and chin short and tiny but her eyes shining down, big and slanting, their blueness dimmed only a little. She smiled. Her big teeth gleamed white in the glossy slate grey.

The elevator at last reached the top floor, the thirtieth, and stopped with a shudder. After the customary long pause the doors slowly opened. Elizabeth stepped out and walked down the long, carpeted corridor to the door on the left at the end. She was now empty of feeling: all the horror had vanished as she stepped, her left foot after the right, over the miniscule gap which even then could quite suddenly widen. She had stepped quickly: she was now, for the time being, safe.

Her thoughts had reverted to the image that was never long out of them. She saw the handsome, broad face and thick, curly hair and those greeny-grey eyes full of love and desire. Soon Bob would be hers.

She pressed the bell. She knew she was expected. The door opened. There appeared on the threshold a tall, thin man, slightly stooped.

'Elizabeth, I'm honoured.' The voice was that slightly wheedling drawl so familiar to her. It held a faint note of nervousness. At the sound of it, and at the sight of the pale blue eyes behind glasses and the invariable half-smile, Elizabeth experienced a sensation she could not have easily named to herself even had she been fully conscious of feeling it. But when Matthew Erikson took a step back to allow her to enter she did not immediately move. There was not quite enough room for her to pass without brushing against him.

'Now you're here won't you come in?' He was staring into her eyes: as always she was fully aware of their power of attraction. He seemed, despite the length of time he had known her and the way in which he had known her, as people invariably seemed, mesmerised by them. She smiled at him with a smile she knew could still have some of the effect it had had in the past.

He blinked quickly three or four times. She laughed and hitched her shoulder bag further up on her shoulder.

'Come on in, Elizabeth.'

'You might wish I hadn't.'

She meant her tone to be light: it came out sombre. She did not know why she had made the remark. She had not planned to. It had been stupid.

'Why, what have you come for?' The nervousness in his

voice had become even stronger. She felt irritated. She knew from her experience of him that it was a nervousness provoked by cowardice and guilt but that it never stood in the way of the satisfaction of a pressing desire.

'You know I always like to see you when I come down here.'

She knew he knew she was lying. His half-smile showed a momentary suggestion of scornfulness but then it was gone. He once more seemed anxious.

'I always like to see *you*. It's been far too long. I've missed you.'

'Like hell.'

'Now, Elizabeth, why do you say that? You know . . .'

'Shut up, Matt.'

For a few moments they looked at each other, unmoving.

He appeared quite unchanged from when she had first met and known him though he had then been a young man and now was an old one. His head and face were so unusually narrow that his features – pale blue eyes, staring without any expression except a flicker of fear behind big, round glasses; long nose; thin-lipped mouth – seemed wide though they were not really wide. There were long, vertical lines down his cheeks. His smile was as always on one side of his mouth as though the other were paralysed. His whole haggard face revealed clearly that he had known many troubles: troubles of soul, not of circumstance. It showed he had entered old age. Yet Elizabeth had no recollection of a younger, less disturbed face.

He held a cigarette down by his side as though he had no present intention of smoking it. The long, trembling fingers between which it hung loosely were stained brown where the smoke had habitually wafted up over them. He wore a shabby jacket whose darkness made the pallor of the skin of his thin neck and face appear even paler. The fairness of his sparse hair faded at the temples and the nape of the neck to the whiteness of age. She did not recall its having ever been otherwise.

But it had never occurred to Elizabeth that he seemed unchanged to her and that this surely was strange when she had known him twenty-five years. It had not occurred to her that the present facade might have been superimposed in her mind on those of the past: that she might have no wish to remember its owner as he had appeared when she had looked at his face and into his eyes long ago.

'Well, well.' His voice was more relaxed now but it still revealed nervousness. He widened the half-smile a little. 'It's been a very long time this time. I'd say nine or ten months.' He moved aside, with a slight bend of the head. She walked quickly past him and he shut the door after her.

The room was all darkened whiteness. The walls and ceiling were white and the furnishings were off-white or beige but the dim light in the room cast a dusky veneer over everything. The window at the far end, the height and width of the wall, was shaded by a venetian blind pulled down to nine-tenths of its length.

Beneath the blind was a slit of blue so uninterrupted and flawless that it seemed painted wall. But it was the sky.

He followed her in and went past, half turning towards her. He walked in that way, slightly awkward and stiff, eternally familiar in Elizabeth's eyes. He gazed at her, obliquely, from behind the big lenses.

'You look very beautiful.'

'Oh, God, Matt, spare me compliments.'

The almost burnt-out cigarette in his fingers trembled a little at this reproof. Elizabeth felt a prick of contempt. He lifted the cigarette to his lips; there was not enough left to draw.

She glanced round the apartment. Nothing seemed changed.

Erikson crossed to the coffee table and leant over it with his back to her. She could tell by the angle of his body and the movements of his narrow, hunched shoulders that he was pushing the stub down and out in the ashtray. As he shifted position a little she saw that he was taking another cigarette from the filled, open box that he kept on the table. He lit it with a long silver lighter, placed as always next to the box. It was like him not to use one cigarette for lighting another. He had not known beforehand he would have another so soon. Had he known, he would not have approved. Elizabeth had not consciously perceived this about him but she was aware of strong irritation at the sight of his actions.

She said, 'Nothing's changed.' She added, again glancing round, explaining her remark to herself as well as to Erikson, 'There's never anything new in here.'

'That's true, there isn't.' He drew on the newly lit cigarette. 'It suits me fine like it is.' He still had not turned round. He quickly continued, his tone showing an effort at warmth, 'What would you like, Elizabeth? Coffee? Coke? A glass of white wine?'

'Coffee.' Elizabeth sat down in one of the two armchairs that were the room's only items of unaltering furniture besides a table with four dining-chairs round it and the coffee table and a bookcase with a stereo system built into it. A large air conditioner, constructed as part of the wall below the right-hand end of the window, hummed vigorously. Erikson went into the kitchenette divided from the room they were in by a wall with no door. In there, out of sight of Elizabeth, his voice when he spoke next had gained a more confident note.

'Is it as hot out there as it was yesterday?'

'It's up in the nineties.'

'Must feel real stifling after the hills.'

'No big difference.' Elizabeth was half-conscious of her annoyance at his referring to the New Dartmouth region as 'the hills' as though it might be any area rural in character north of the City. Holding the chair arms with her hands to give herself leverage, she shifted her buttocks back in the chair, first one, then the other. Then she sat up straight and folded one ankle over its fellow, her legs on a slant. She patted her hair and pushed a strayed lock back with the rest, from over her eyebrow.

At least Matthew's apartment was cool. The sweat that had covered her out in the street had now dried. She felt confident that her appearance was still as immaculate as she could desire. She again glanced round the room. A lot could be done to it. But he had never cared about where he was living beyond simple neatness. She remembered his long, thin body stretched out in an armchair with his feet on a footstool as he read some textbook, oblivious of the unsightly brown walls and the schlocky cheap reproductions of second-rate paintings.

He came round the side of the wall with two cups. He gave her one of them and sat down with the other in the second armchair. He must have finished or abandoned the cigarette he had just lit. He looked at her, blinking, then looked away. He picked his spoon up from his saucer, put it into his coffee and began to rotate it, slowly and evenly. He seemed to retain some, if not much, of the confidence he had gained when out of her sight. He lifted the spoon, suspending it upright a moment and then shaking it over the cup. He laid it down in his saucer and said, with a nervous brusqueness that an attempt at heartiness could not conceal, 'Well, Elizabeth, why have you come?'

Elizabeth felt a disagreeable churn of the stomach. She knew though that she had allowed nothing to show on her face.

'I'll get to it.' She lifted her cup from the saucer she held in her lap and took a sip of her coffee.

'In no hurry to tell me, huh? I wonder what it can be.' His tone was now so full of nervousness as to be close to one of alarm.

Elizabeth slightly altered the slant of her legs, dipping her knees so that thighs and calves formed a more acute angle. She noticed Matthew observe this. She pulled down her skirt as far as it went, which was to the end of but not over the top of her knees.

'Is it something I'm not gonna like?' His pale eyes seemed huge in his thin face behind his big glasses.

'Maybe.'

'Well, O.K., I'm in no hurry, Elizabeth.' He cleared his throat. 'Take your time.'

Elizabeth put her coffee cup back down on her saucer. She again glanced round the room, then looked backed at Matthew.

'Have you appointed the new manager yet?'

He looked surprised. The question clearly did not meet the expectations he had formed as to what she might say. His momentarily open expression became again wary.

'How did you know I was looking for one?'

'Wayne told me.'

'What would Wayne go telling you that for?'

'I guess he thought it might interest me.'

'Why should it interest you?'

'I'll tell you why in a minute. First answer my questions.'

'Are you and Wayne still . . .'

'That's none of your business.'

'I guess you see a lot of him, now he's Dick partner.'

'I told you Matt it's none of your business.'

'He seems to be happy enough to discuss my affairs with you.'

'It's hardly some dark secret you want a new manager.'

'All the same . . .'

'Be glad Wayne's your friend. He's not a good person to have as an enemy.' She laughed.

'I thought you still liked him.'

'I like him a lot.'

'I treated him well when *he* was my manager.'

'He didn't stay long.'

'He seemed to think the architecture business might suit him better than pharmacy. It was what he was originally trained for.'

'Yeah. Anyway, he learned a thing or two about the pharmacist, didn't he?'

'Why d'you want to know if I've got a new manager?'

'Like I said, first answer my question. There's no reason not to. I could find out from Wayne easy enough.'

'No I haven't found anyone yet as it happens. It's not a

straightforward thing finding someone you can trust in this line. The last manager . . .'

Her attention lapsed. She heard not a word more as he continued to talk on the topic of managers. It did not occur to her that he was avoiding both what might be to come and what had been touched on a moment before. She did not reflect on his possible motives or feelings. She thought ahead about what she would say next till she suddenly realised he had gone silent. She recaptured his gaze, aware as always of the power of her eyes to take and keep hold of another's when and for as long as she pleased.

'So you're running the business yourself now?'

'For the time being I am.'

There was a short pause. Elizabeth was once again rehearsing in her mind her prepared statement and question. He said, 'If you want drugs I can't help you. I can't risk it. Not even for you, Liz.'

'I don't want drugs. Not the kind you mean anyway.' Her prepared remarks came out faster and shorter than she had intended. 'I want some sleeping pill that'll dissolve in a drink. I want it today.'

Erikson stared at her. His eyes seemed huge and pale behind his large glasses. They had made Elizabeth think long ago of two over-sized marbles floating just under water and this image occurred to her again now, rather surprising her. She was only dimly aware that it was not a new thought but a memory. The eyes showed little expression beyond the same glimmer of fear that had been in them when he had opened the door. There was perhaps a hint of surprise in them also. He drained his coffee, put down his cup on the table and reached for a cigarette and the lighter. He lit up and said, 'I'd have to know what you want it for.'

Elizabeth put her cup and saucer down on the floor, stood up and walked to the window. She pushed the blind up an inch or two and gazed out at the sky. It was in its blueness unflawed and impenetrable. She looked down at the children's playground so far below that the people in it seemed smaller than dolls, smaller even than insects: mere moving specks. To the right were the railway tracks and beyond them the river. Down along it were piers with more specks, this time immobile. It occurred to her that they were dotted around like amphibious creatures on rocks and almost simultaneously that they were laid out as on slabs. These thoughts suddenly cohered in her mind with the phrase 'sunbathing or dead'. She gave a brief laugh. Beyond, far in the distance, on the horizon, was the eternally familiar raised female arm, as small as a pin, bearing a torch.

She turned again to face into the room, leaving the blind as it was. Matthew Erikson had moved round in his seat and was looking towards her, glasses glinting, eyes half-closed into slits.

'Something funny out there?'

'No, nothing funny.'

He kept staring at her. 'How did you get here? By car? Where did you park it?'

'I came down by bus.'

'Really? I wouldn't have thought you'd want to do that. You get all sorts of unsavoury characters using those buses.'

There was a long pause. Elizabeth stared at him: his thin face slowly contorted till it wore an agonised look. She felt a mild, remote satisfaction. She crossed to her chair and sat down. Then she picked up her cup and saucer and brought them to her lap and leant back, again crossing her ankles.

'You don't need to know why I want it.'

He gave a deep sigh and stubbed out what was left of his cigarette. Slowly, with a considerable amount of adjusting of trouser at shin, knee and crotch, he stretched his legs out in front of him.

'Things have changed. I'm an old man now. I don't care any more what anyone knows, even supposing you made them believe it.'

'Don't you? Like hell. Imagine Wayne knowing. I'd have no trouble there. He'd believe it. The police would probably believe it as well. You'd care all right when they started turning up evidence.'

'There's no evidence.'

'I'm sure you'd prefer it if nobody tried to find out if you're right about that.'

'There's no evidence.' He stood up. He turned away from her, shuffled a step or two forward, turned back, leant over the table, took a cigarette, paused a moment and then sat down again on his chair.

He said, staring ahead of him, 'I may not have very much longer to live.'

Elizabeth laughed.

'You think that's funny, Elizabeth?' He did not look at her.

'I won't think it's funny if you show me the doctors' bills.'

'There'll be doctors' bills soon enough.'

'There aren't any yet, though.'

He placed the unlit cigarette on the table.

'I'm not giving you a sleeping pill or anything else till I know why.'

'I'm not telling you why.'

'Then I'm not giving you anything. Go to a doctor and get a prescription.'

'For a sleeping pill that dissolves without giving any colour or taste to the drink? No doctor would even know what to prescribe, only pharmacists have access to that sort of stuff.'

'I'm not giving you anything till you give me a reason.'

They sat for a while in silence. Erikson picked up the cigarette and proceeded to light it, Elizabeth watching him. She did not show it but she felt consternation. His air, as he sat there, was surprisingly obstinate.

He stood up again, holding his cigarette, not looking her way.

'I think you might as well go.'

She gazed up at him. His stance was quite confident. His mind seemed made up. Was he truly past caring? Or did he simply know she would have to give way? That if she used her information against him, she would lose all her power? That she wanted what she wanted too much not to risk telling him what she intended to do? She did not know how to answer these questions. However long and hard she gazed into his face his thoughts stayed unknown to her.

'I said you might as well go.'

'I'll go when I want to go.'

Erikson sighed and sat down again.

'Look, why don't I help you to tell me, Elizabeth.' He leant forwards. 'It'll probably be better for both of us in the end. I'd like to help you if I can. You know I'm fond of you.'

'Yeah? Well, I don't see how you can help me to tell you. I'm not going to tell you.'

'I've nothing against getting you whatever you want if I can do it without any risk to myself.' He paused, then went on, 'Who d'you want to drug, Elizabeth?'

She did not answer.

'What d'you want to do to them while they're asleep?'

'I told you, it's nothing you need know about.'

'Don't forget if I'm to get what you need I have to know how quickly you want it to work. I also have to know how deep a sleep you want the person to go into.'

'It has to work straightaway.'

'Straightaway?'

'Like an anaesthetic. Instantly.'

'Then it's no sleeping pill you need. It's a knock-out pill. Or, more likely, a powder or potion. I'd have to concoct that for you myself.'

'You could do that.'

'Sure I could. But I'd have to know why.' He paused, then continued, leaning forwards a little, his mouth twisted into a tiny half-smile, 'D'you want this powder in order to kill someone? To knock them out and then kill them?'

Elizabeth found herself sweating quite suddenly. It struck her as curious when the room was so cool.

'Who is it you want to kill, Elizabeth, Dick?'

She laughed.

'No,' he said. 'Dick's not worth the killing.'

'Shut up.'

'You've got all you want out of Dick, you and Wayne.

You've both got the use of his money. Poor old Dick. You don't need to kill him. All right, Elizabeth, no need to look as though it was me you wanted to kill.' He paused for a moment. 'Perhaps it is.'

'No, I don't want to kill you. Not enough to risk going to prison.'

'Who is it, then? Tell me who and why and how you plan doing it and I'll give you the drug. That is as long as your plan seems sufficiently foolproof. I have to be sure there's no risk. I have to be certain the drug won't be traced back to me. I have to be certain no one knows you've come here today.'

It did not take her long to decide to tell him the truth. She guessed now that he was as much in fear of detection – and of a possible trial and conviction – as ever. But he wanted something on her as she had something on him. Until she gave him that he was not going to help her. He must know that she would not throw away all her power over him at this stage by telling Wayne, or the police, or anyone else, about his friendship with the ten-year-old who had disappeared and whose body, two weeks later, had been found in the Hudson.

'All right, I'll tell you. I'm in love with someone who loves me too but won't leave his wife. He's a Catholic. If I get rid of his wife and divorce Dick he'll marry me.'

'How are you planning to do it?'

'It's very simple. She has a patio overlooking a hundred-foot drop at the back of her house. I send her to sleep and then push her over. It'll look exactly like suicide.'

'Has she got any reason for wanting to kill herself?'

'A very good reason. Her husband's business is about to go bust. They'll lose everything.'

'How d'you know that?'

'Dick told me. That is, Dick told me Bob had borrowed some money from him to tide the business over during the next couple of days. It looks to me like Bob's kidding himself, thinking Dick's loan will bale him out. It looks to me like the business is going to go under.'

'It looks to *you*. But does it look like that to her?

Anyway, it seems a pretty flimsy motive for suicide. Surely Dick doesn't think the business is going to go under. He'd hardly lend Bob the money if he did.'

'Dick just believed every word Bob said to him.'

'He doesn't sound a very good prospect, your Bob.'

'That doesn't worry me. I'll have money enough with what Dick has to give me and Bob can start over.'

'Was this a large loan Dick made?'

'He wouldn't tell me exactly but I gathered it was. It was an incredibly stupid thing to have done. But the house and property are worth a small fortune. Half the value of those will set me up fine.'

'I won't do it, Elizabeth. It all sounds too risky. It'll look like possible murder and you'll be a suspect.'

'That's absurd. It won't occur to anyone it wasn't a suicide.'

'Sure it will, when you and Bob got married right afterwards.'

'We won't get married right afterwards. I have to get divorced first.'

'If there's an autopsy they'd find the remains of the drug in her stomach. They'd know it was no ordinary sleeping pill.'

'If they don't suspect foul play there won't be an autopsy. Anyway, just supposing there was, they couldn't trace the drug back to me and if they did they couldn't know I got it from you. I came down today on the bus so I wouldn't need to park the car anywhere round here.'

'I didn't know there was a bus down from where you are on a Sunday.'

'Yeah. The one-thirty. I'll get the six-thirty back. I decided to come down as soon as Dick told me what Bob had asked him this morning. It occurred to me instantly it meant a motive for suicide. Dick thinks I'm shopping.'

'On a *Sunday*?'

'There's plenty of shops open on Sunday.'

'There's plenty not open.'

'I'll go back with shopping, don't worry.'

'Have you ever before come down to the City to shop on a Sunday?'

'No, but Dick isn't likely to question it. Look, don't worry. No one'll ever find out I've been here to see you.'

'The doorman saw you.'

'I gave him a false name and sailed right past. It was a new doorman since I was here the last time I came, he'd never seen me before, he hardly glanced at me, he'd never know me again.'

'Everyone glances at you. I can't believe he wouldn't know you again.'

'I didn't look at him directly. He didn't show any interest. Maybe he was gay.'

'The whole scheme's too risky. I don't want to be part of it.'

Elizabeth knew Matthew was wrong about the degree of the risk. Whenever she made up her mind to do something and planned it carefully it always went right for her. There were occasional setbacks: Beattie had realised a moment too soon the pool was empty of water. But she had hatched that idea on the spur of the moment, when the men had left the dining room for the den after dinner.

She had at first quite innocently thought she and Beattie might go for a swim: she had then remembered Dick was to have emptied the pool: she had envisaged herself, with momentary horror, diving off the board above nothing but concrete; the small figure she saw in her mind, as it fell towards death, had turned into Beattie – and in a flash she had arrived at her scheme. The details, such as sending Beattie ahead of her and then delaying switching the lights on, had come to her within moments.

If it had not been for that ridiculously loose-fitting bracelet the plan would have worked perfectly.

Admittedly the previous scheme had misfired too. It might still have worked out, if Beattie had not come back too early that Saturday morning. At least Elizabeth had been careful and had not been caught doing anything strange or suspicious. It had been annoying that Beattie had noticed the scratches. She had had a lot of trouble lifting the stone under which that rattlesnake had been coiled. It had taken her a shorter time than she had expected to find it. It was just what she wanted, a healthy, fully-grown specimen. She had been lucky. Rattlesnakes were not particularly rare in this area but they were not common either. It had been at the very edge of the clearing, where the grass and weeds began thickening to undergrowth. But she had been unlucky in that it had slithered and wriggled away before she could properly grasp it and get it into the box she had brought from her house. She had left that in the field and gone on to Beattie's. She had wanted to have a look round, to decide on exactly where she would let the snake out, so that it would be likely to attack Beattie when she came home. Afterwards she would return to the forest and look for it again, or find another one. She had fixed on a corner of the studio, behind one of the canvases, as the best place to put it, when she heard Beattie's car.

She had had to leave the box where it was, out in the field on Bob and Beattie's land at the edge of the forest. But it was not likely to be discovered. It was cardboard: it would merge in time into the earth.

But these were temporary failures. She knew very well that she always got her way in the end. She had a special, it seemed God-given, power to get what she wanted. She had not prayed, since she was a child, to the Lutheran God she had been brought up to believe in. But she had never entirely ceased to credit either His existence or His interest in Elizabeth Andersen. She believed He was backing her. In a deeper part of her mind she knew she was defying His laws and the laws of every land on earth and every god in the sky; but that knowledge, along with all the other unbearable knowing, was hidden.

And she wanted Bob as she had never wanted anything before in her life. She had once wanted Wayne: she had taken possession of him, as a lover, without trouble; when her desire for him ceased they had stayed allies and friends. They were bound by shared interest and knowledge: of

Matthew; of Dick; of each other. She was closer to him than to anyone. He understood her. He had said to her, often, 'Go for what you want, Elizabeth. No one else is gonna do it for you. It's every man for himself in this world. And woman.' He had helped her overcome the last of her scruples about marrying Dick for his money.

But Elizabeth wanted Bob differently from the way she wanted, or had ever wanted, anything else. She believed that if he were her husband her life would become something quite altered from what it was now. It would be filled again with emotions she had ceased feeling twenty years earlier: pleasure; enjoyment; delight; tender love.

She knew he wanted her. He did not love Beattie. He could not. She was not lovable. She was scrawny. She was sallow and plain and sharp-tongued. She treated him coldly. She made his life miserable.

Elizabeth on the other hand was all a man could ever want in a wife. And she loved him with passion. She would make him blissfully happy. She had a right to him.

But she had the strong impression Matthew meant what he said about the risk of the scheme. She guessed she would be unable to persuade him that it was as negligible as she herself knew it to be. That air of obstinacy about him was all too familiar. She knew now that he would be obdurate in the face of all her pleas and cajolery. She had to find another line of attack if she was to get what she wanted. She thought hard for a while.

'There'll be something in it for you. As well as my not telling your secrets.'

'Oh, yes? What could that be?'

'He has a ten-year-old daughter.'

'Ah.'

'So will you get me the drug?'

'What is it you're promising me?'

'She means nothing to me. Her father need never know anything.'

'Are you saying that once you're married to this man you'll invite me up to spend time with the three of you regularly and I'll be able to enjoy this little girl's company as much as I like?'

'Sure. I'll even arrange for her to come and stay with you down here in the City. Why not? No one's ever going to suspect if I don't tell them anything.'

He reached for his packet of cigarettes and lit one with a hand shaking more than ever.

'She's a gorgeous girl, Matt.' Elizabeth gazed at him, her eyes at their widest. 'Tall for her age. Well built.'

Erikson took a long breath. Elizabeth left her seat and came up to him. She knelt on the floor beside him, looking up, fixing his eyes with her own. 'Shall I tell you about her?'

She put her hand on his thigh.

Later, in the bathroom, throwing up again and again in the washbasin, holding her hair away from her mouth, she felt strange, intense jubilation and kept repeating the words in her mind, 'Now it's done, now I'll get what I want.' Her failures were behind her: it was time now for success.

Chapter Nine

THERE had been an angry silence between them all day. When Bob came down to the kitchen Beattie was dressed in her wide skirt and suntop, her hair up in a bun, scouring the sink. The kitchen was immaculate: she was clearly completing a full-scale cleaning job. Since it was a Sunday morning, still early, this was an extremely bad sign. He asked about breakfast: she did not answer; he asked whether she was still angry: she walked out of the kitchen.

Later he heard her on the phone making plans to collect Melly from Barbara's just before lunch. When he was crossing the hall on his way out of the house, dressed in a suit ready for church, he stopped at the door to the sitting room and peered in to where Beattie was vigorously polishing a table. She gave no sign of observing his presence. Her back was straight as a rod, her face thin and haggard, her jaw tight. He said that he would pick up their daughter on his way home. He pointed out that the timing would be about right. Beattie assented by giving a brief, expressionless nod. He said again that he was sorry for what had happened last night. She said calmly and coldly that it wasn't just that. What else was it? he asked her. He would have preferred not to ask but the question was clearly required of him. In any case things could not be much longer left as they were. He said if only she'd tell him he could try to put everything right. She said he knew perfectly well what was wrong. He said in a tone of unease, with a chill at his heart, he did not. She then said she did not want to talk about it right now and he had better go or he would be late for the service.

Had circumstances been rather different he would have lost his temper at her dismissal. He would probably have done so in an uncontrolled, violent manner. As it was, he left the house quietly.

He went not to church but to see Dick.

Melly struck him as taller and bigger than even a week ago when, a couple of hours later, he walked into Barbara's kitchen where she was seated at the long pine table eating a sizeable snack. Barbara's daughter Tabitha sat next to her feeding more frugally from a bag of potato chips.

'Daddy! Daddy! Daddy!'

His reception by Melly concurred with his fondest imagining. She was ecstatic. A glass of milk and a chair were knocked over: he himself staggered a little though he managed not to fall down.

'Melly . . .' He hugged her close, glorying in the love she was showing him. He knew Barbara was watching: he felt elated and proud. He kissed his daughter all over her forehead and cheeks.

'My Daddy . . .'

'I've missed you terribly, pumpkin.'

He was filled full with love for her: it hurt him, as though he felt glancingly, as one might feel the stirring of air that presages a hurricane, the agony that this love would produce were she to die.

'You shouldn't have stayed away for so long.' She was already pouting even as she was only that moment beginning to lessen the strength of her grip. Her adoration of him came often like this, in waves that ebbed into defiance and anger but flowed back again to climb high and then crash noisily over him in hugging and endearments and kisses.

'I couldn't help it. D'you think I'd have stayed away for a week or even a night if I could have avoided it? I had to, Melly, I'd never be away from you and Mommy by choice.'

She stared up at him. Her narrow hazel eyes and puffed cheeks showed a momentarily neutral expression. The wave was retreating, but this time to apparent detachment rather than mutiny.

'Mommy and I went to see *The Lost Aliens from the Centre of the Universe.*'

'Was it good?'

'Pretty good.'

The wave flowed back quickly and violently. She threw herself at him again.

'Daddy, Daddy, Daddy.'

'I'll be with you all weekend now.' He beamed down at her, stroking her hair as she hugged his waist and gazed adoringly up at him. 'This afternoon I'll take you to the beach. How about that? We'll get there in time for the ice cream van. Would you like to go with Daddy to the beach and swim together out to the raft and eat an ice cream cone? We might even go to the pizza hut and have one of those onion and pepperoni pizzas you're crazy about.' He knew he might have sounded to other ears – including Beattie's ears – over-indulgent; he did not care: he felt proud of his love for his child.

Melly relaxed her hold. Her look again became neutral.

'O.K., sure.' She considered a moment. 'Also, can I have five dollars to get the poster of *The Lost Aliens from the Centre of the Universe*? They've got it in the Maple Tree bookstore but Mommy wouldn't buy it for me, she said to ask you.' She delivered these words, her voice surprisingly deep and slow for a child of ten, in a flat, matter of fact tone with great force behind it. It was reminiscent of Beattie's tone in certain moods without being a copy. It was a timbre Beattie used when displeased or determined, without the clothing of detachment or charm or vivacity. It was Beattie's tone naked, Bob caught the echo of Beattie's voice as it had sounded last night when she had said, 'That was barbaric'. He quenched the memory.

'Yeah, I'll give you five dollars.'

A surge of panic was rising. But he remembered: he had a way out.

Melly said, 'You've stayed away *too long*.'

In the car she continued by turns to go into raptures and to needle him.

When they walked into the house Beattie spoke only to Melly except to ask Bob why they were so late getting back. She had had lunch ready for nearly an hour. He said he had stayed chatting to Barbara. He hoped, not securely, that neither Melly that day, nor Barbara at some later time, would purposely or accidentally expose this deception.

The two adults and child sat round the long kitchen table and ate tuna fish and salad, both parents talking separately to their composed, deep-voiced daughter, quite often as part of the same conversation. They spoke not at all to each other. Bob felt thankful that Melly's appetite was such that she was able to eat a good lunch though she had just had the snack. That late morning sandwich would have given away that he had been seriously late in getting to Barbara's.

After lunch Bob drove Melly to the Lake Tocahoe beach: Beattie stayed home. The parking area was so crowded that Bob had to drive out of it and back down the road and do a U-turn and then drive back in again. Even so he had to park in a spot, almost blocking another car, that he had, first time round, deemed unsuitable.

Bob and Melly installed themselves in the family's usual spot, on the far side from the fence. Bob set up a chair and

Melly spread out a towel. They took off their clothes: both were wearing their swimsuits under their T-shirts and shorts. Then they walked together through the crowds spread over the sand to the edge of the water. The water was warm. They were soon immersed and swimming side by side to the raft down the lake. Melly swam well; she was almost as strong a swimmer as Bob.

Later, as Bob had promised, they bought some ice cream from the van that drew up just outside the beach, playing a tune. After that Melly met a schoolfriend and played for a while in the sand. Bob sat in the chair, the Sunday papers spread out on his knees.

He pictured Beattie's angry, set face. He felt a sense of injustice but when he remembered what had happened last night it dissolved. He tried to decide what he should do to ease the tension between the two of them but the subject was too difficult and painful to hold his attention for more than a minute. He saw her in his mind's eye as she had looked last night at dinner: so attractive, in her new blouse and those white, dangling earrings. He remembered her later that evening running into Dick's den, unkempt, eyes enormous, shaking with terror. He quickly banished the image.

He thought again of his and Dick's plan. He felt warily thankful for the relief Dick had given him. He believed all his problems now would be solved. He needed only to exercise some care and ingenuity in using the money.

He glanced at the papers and greeted people he knew as they passed and gazed at the beautiful view down the lake to the purple and blue and green hills.

The fear was still there underneath but much lessened. He believed all – business, house, their life up here in New Dartmouth – now would be saved.

Bob did not take Melly back home till past six. She at once settled herself in front of the television. Bob sat a long way from the set in the huge room, still nursing the papers. But despite the distance his eye was drawn to the pro-gramme Melly was watching, in which a group of three men

and a girl were stalking and apparently out-witting a crimi-
nal. Cartoon characters, he thought. But he found himself
continuing to watch despite his scorn and aversion.

After a while Beattie brought Melly's supper, putting it
on the small table next to her. Melly began eating, hardly
taking her eyes off the screen.

Beattie addressed Bob directly for the first time since his
and Melly's return from the beach.

'D'you want yours now also?'

Bob was hungry. Melly's pasta smelled good. He realised he did rather want his now. In any case he did not
foresee, later this evening, a companionable candlelit supper
such as he and Beattie usually ate when both were at home.
He presumed that, one way or another, Beattie would this
evening so arrange things as to make sure they ate separately. All the same he said, 'What about you? When are you
having yours?'

'I'm not.'

'You're not having supper?'

'No.'

He felt strong displeasure: Beattie's reluctance to eat
always displeased him. It displeased him still more when the
reluctance was caused by resentment and anger and intended to hurt him. However, for once, he did not take up
the issue.

'O.K.'

'What does O.K. mean? O.K. you'll have yours now?'

'Yeah.'

She brought him his pasta and salad – helpings of both
so enormous as, Bob felt, to be obscurely insulting – on a
large wooden tray. Despite the mild indignity of eating his
meal on his knees, as though he were a child or invalid, he
did not make any objection to the unusual arrangement. The
food proved delicious. Beattie was an excellent cook, despite
her own lack of interest in eating. He finished his two
platefuls, still watching the programme. This at last reached
its predictable conclusion. There was a top-full glass of red
wine next to his pasta, which he drank rather quickly. He

felt he could do with some – or even perhaps quite a lot – more.

Beattie reappeared and took the tray from his knees with the air of a cafeteria waitress who has had a specially taxing and difficult day. Bob, still holding his wine glass, got up and followed her out to the kitchen. He said, 'That was delicious' but she appeared not to hear. Then he said, 'Could I have another glass of that wine?'

'Help yourself. The bottle's in that cupboard.' She pointed, and then turned to the sink.

He decided that this was not yet the moment to attempt a *rapprochement*.

But when Melly was in bed, much later that evening, Bob at last took the initiative. Beattie was putting some culinary items, most of which he could not have identified, in a kitchen closet, already well stocked, as part of a sorting and tidying process she had embarked on. He reached up to move a few gadgets or tools from one shelf to another to assist her. Then he took the thing she was holding and wedged it into the space thus created. The thing was large, round, plastic and complicated, its purpose quite unimaginable.

'What is it?'

'A tomato cutter.'

'What's it got that a knife hasn't?'

'It makes pretty shapes.'

He put his arms round her, kissed her forehead and said, 'I want to hear what I've done. I can't bear this . . . *estrangement*.' Underneath his carefully established facade of calm and maturity he did not feel calm at all. He dreaded what he might hear. But it seemed to him that the silence between them was worse even than anything she might be going to say.

They went into the sitting room and sat on the sofa together. Bob put his arm round her shoulder. She did not respond to his touch but sat slightly hunched, looking straight ahead of her, her expression resolved. He asked her again what was wrong.

Gradually, taking her time, Beattie outlined the grudges she was holding against him. The first was his barbaric behaviour of yesterday. Bob again said he was sorry but that he had not meant any harm but all the same he understood how she felt and, again, he was sorry. The second was his reluctance to tell her what was wrong with the business. He repeated that he had wanted to forget about it when he came home but that he had said yesterday he would tell her today and he would. The third was his refusal to take seriously the claim that Elizabeth had tried to kill her the evening before, or even to listen with proper attention to her – Beattie's – reasons for making it. He said he would listen again, this time more carefully. The fourth was his denial, which she knew in advance he would give, of the request she had intended to make, and now was making, that he should stay up in New Dartmouth tomorrow to protect her from further attempts on her life.

By the time she had finished with her fourth cause of annoyance they were an inch or two further apart than they had been. Beattie was still looking ahead of her. Bob's arm had moved from her shoulders and lay along the back of the sofa.

Though Bob had offered to listen again to Beattie's reasons for thinking yesterday's near fatal accident had been attempted cold-blooded murder he had to concede that, whatever she might say, he could not stay home the next morning. She asked him to tell her what was so wrong with the business that it demanded more urgent attention than his wife's, and perhaps his child's, physical safety.

After a few moments' thought Bob gave her an edited account of his cash flow problems. He told her nothing of the transaction with Dick. Beattie listened in silence. He knew very well she was fully aware that there was much left unsaid. He found himself rambling a little. He was sweating.

When he stopped speaking she remained silent a moment. Then she said quietly that she still did not believe it was impossible for him to stay in New Dartmouth the following day.

There was a short pause. Then Bob said he could not miss his planned meetings. She did not reply.

After a while he went on to say that he was convinced she was not in real danger. She had overreacted to what had happened last night. She was prejudiced against Elizabeth Andersen. She had become paranoid about her.

This last remark, as he knew the minute he made it, was a mistake. Beattie got up from the sofa and walked out of the room. She did not speak to him again for the rest of the evening.

Two or three times he was on the point of trying to persuade her to do so but then he felt he could not go through with it.

Beattie went to bed early. When he at last got in beside her she was turned away from his side, fast asleep.

Chapter
Ten

ELIZABETH drove out from the trees, onto the wide space in front of the house set against sky. The engine sounded unnaturally loud as she drew her car up beside Beattie's and braked. She switched off the ignition and found herself alone with her thoughts and intentions in what now seemed an unnaturally undisturbed quietness.

She climbed out of the car, her bag over her shoulder, carrying the small cardboard packet with red Chinese lettering that had lain on the passenger seat. She guessed Beattie must by now know someone was here. In a moment she would come from the house.

The silence had now filled with birdsong and a humming of something mechanical at a very great distance and the buzz of a plane. These sounds did not join in a gentle outdoor cacophony: each stayed separate. Elizabeth stood listening a moment. The sounds seemed menacing. No one noise in itself suggested a threat. But they were together part of that whole outdoor world against which she had set herself, that seemed made up of danger.

As she closed the car door and began to walk to the house the sweat poured off her body. She held in her hand the packet of tea. The cardboard felt sticky.

Elizabeth had never known heat so intense. Or rather, she had never felt heat so intensely. Even in the car, with the air conditioning on, she had sweated: she had shivered a little as the dampness dried on her skin. She had sweated all morning except for a moment or two after her shower: the dampness was on her again within moments after she had rubbed herself dry and put on her clothes. And all the previous night she had lain naked without sheets or blankets in a hot, rancid wetness. It had seemed the longest night of her life. She had seemed never quite to sink into slumber yet was constantly dreaming.

When she woke it was with a sense of surprise that she *could* wake: that she had slept after all. She had lain for a minute or two half-bewildered. She had been aware of the sun's brightness and heat pressed through the wide-open window and yet she still saw before her a dark, twisted tree with no leaves. A black branch stood out from the grey of the rest. It was of a rough, pitted texture with sharp, hurting twigs. Its wood was damp to the touch but with a dampness not watery but viscous. She saw a patch of dark earth with some plant roots or undergrowth on it. As the dreaming eye came up close to the patch it perceived, half emerged from the roots, a coiled, dead snake.

Elizabeth walked through the garden towards the front of the house. It showed nothing but sky-blank windows and, in the shadowy porch, the closed door. She wondered if Beattie had gone for one of her rambles. She walked on into the shade. But then she looked round, in the direction she had come from, and glimpsed a figure off to one side on the left. She turned to face him or her. It was Beattie, coming rapidly round the side of the house. She was wearing a wide skirt and red suntop and a sunhat.

Elizabeth moved quickly, almost running, towards her. 'Beattie!'

Beattie did not smile. She stopped walking and put her hand to the crown of her hat.

Elizabeth came up to her.

'Beattie, I feel so guilty about what happened Saturday? I wanted to come up and say how sorry I was?'

Beattie said nothing. She still did not smile.

'I guess you're still mad at me. I wouldn't blame you. I'd feel the same. Of course it was nobody's fault but it was a terrible thing to have happened. It was real shocking. We could both have been killed. I'm not surprised you're still mad at me, it's natural, anyone would be.'

'I'm not mad,' Beattie said.

Elizabeth continued smiling as hard as she could.

'Gee, I'm real glad to hear that. I thought maybe when it happened it seemed like I didn't care much but I did, only I was just so shocked I don't know what to say to you . . .'

'Right.'

'Look, I tell you what I've done, Beattie, I've brought something for you, a gift.' She held up the packet, softened with dampness where her hand had been gripping it.

'It's that tea you told me about, Beattie? Ling's Pekinese? I was down in the City and saw it in the window of Zabar's and remembered you said you can't get it up here and thought, hey, I'll get that for Beattie. I thought, I'll take it to her tomorrow.'

Beattie stared at the packet of tea.

'I'm *longing* to try it myself. I thought, my heavens, I wonder what it *tastes* like since Beattie loves it so. We'll have some now. I'll go in and make it for you.'

Beattie gazed back at her now with a look in her eyes that Elizabeth took to be wonder.

'Sure, Beattie, I'll make it. I've made tea before, I know how to do it, with the teapot and all. You go back and sit on your beautiful patio. That's where you were before, right?

That's where you were coming from? I'll find everything in your kitchen without any trouble, I'll bring the tea out to you.'

'No.'

'Why not?'

'I don't want any tea.'

'Well, let me just come and sit with you for a while. Maybe we'll have some tea later.'

'I'm going indoors.'

'Why not go do whatever you have to, then come back out?'

'I'm about to start working.'

'It's too hot to work.'

'I work fine in the heat.'

'It's too hot for *anybody* to work. I've taken the day off from the gallery.'

'I don't mind it this way.'

'Well, I tell you, I'm sure feeling warm.'

Beattie's glance flicked down Elizabeth's body and up again to her face.

'You *look* warm.'

Elizabeth's confidence faltered. But she caught Beattie's gaze and stared into those greeny-grey eyes: she saw them wide open and blank and falling away into darkness. Then she saw Bob's in their place as they had looked at her, with love and desire, on that day he came to her house unexpectedly nine months before, and her resolution returned.

'Have you ever *known* heat like this?'

'Too hot for tea, I'd have said.'

Elizabeth's confidence faltered again but for only a second.

'I'll make iced tea.'

'I have to start working.'

'Take a break.'

'I've had a break. Now I have to start working.'

'There's something I want to discuss with you.'

'Some other time.'

'It can't wait.'

'Yes it can.'

'It's about the business.'

'What business?'

'Bob's business.'

Beattie stared at her and blinked rapidly, again with a look of surprise.

'It'll interest you, Beattie.'

'What have you heard?'

'Go sit on the patio and I'll make the tea and come out and tell you.'

'You go sit on the patio. *I'll* make the tea.'

Beattie reached with her thin arm for the packet.

'No, Beattie, I'll do it.' Elizabeth jerked her arm down by her side. The two women were staring into each other's eyes: Elizabeth saw them again with the life taken out of them, no longer a bar to her and Bob's happiness, to the way things ought to be. She would not give way before Beattie. She would achieve what she had come for. She would do away with this woman. The world would be better without her. She caused nothing but misery.

She took a deep, long breath and re-formed her wide smile.

'Now Beattie, I feel real bad about what happened, I want to make up to you for it, I'll make the tea while you go and relax.' She walked quickly past Beattie, opened the door to the house, went in and made for the kitchen.

But Beattie was following her.

Beattie said, 'Iced tea takes too long. If you really want tea I'll make hot tea.'

'I'll make it.'

Elizabeth began trying to find what she needed. She opened one or two cupboards. She saw saucepans, knives and forks, plates, a bag full of rubbish. Beattie took over. She moved quickly. She put the kettle on to boil and speedily assembled everything needed.

Elizabeth stood helpless, gazing round her. The kitchen was light and immaculate, with pine furniture and gleaming white fittings and with a vase of pretty cut flowers.

Her confidence once again faltered.

But she suddenly realised she could take advantage of this turn of events. As Beattie was pouring water into the teapot she opened her bag, took a tissue out and at the same time removed the packet of powder Matthew had given her.

The amount of powder was enough, Matthew had promised, to put anyone out in a moment. Yet the packet was so small that she could hold it unseen in her hand.

She thought she would have no chance to put it in Beattie's tea while they were still in the house. She hoped and planned to find some way of doing it out on the patio.

But by great good luck the phone rang when Beattie had finished making the tea, Beattie hurried out of the kitchen. Moments later she came back, saying, 'Damn it, I'll leave it . . . It can't be important . . .' but by that time Elizabeth had slipped the powder into one of the cups and picked up the other and was safely across the room at the window, gazing out at the wonderful steep valley view.

They went out to the patio.

It had been a little cooler indoors. Outside, though the patio was at this time of day in the shade, the air seemed almost unbearably hot. Elizabeth was again sweating. She felt afraid Beattie would want to go back indoors. But Beattie showed no sign of being aware of the heat. She put her untasted glass on the table and sat down in one of the white garden chairs. The kitten, who had been mewing at her to try to get her attention, leapt into her lap, curled round and lay down.

Elizabeth sat down in the opposite chair with her cup in her hand. She took a sip.

'Oh, my, it's *delicious*.'

'O.K., what have you heard?'

'Try it, Beattie.'

'In a minute. I want to know what you've heard.'

'Well, Beattie, I'm sure you know already about the business being in trouble. I was so sorry to hear it, I thought, my, how could that happen to two such wonderful people, it just isn't fair, they don't deserve it, Bob's worked so hard.'

'Is that all of it? That it's in trouble?'

'I don't know how much you already know.'

'Try me.'

'I guess you know Bob has cash flow problems.'

'Sure.'

'Maybe you don't know how bad they are.'

'I know they're bad.'

'I guess though maybe you don't know just *how* bad. Maybe Bob hasn't told you. Did you know the business is in danger of folding real soon?'

Beattie sat, one hand on the kitten's soft back, showing no feeling.

'Is that it?' she asked, after a pause.

'Yeah, more or less.'

But Beattie seemed to have no intention of drinking her tea till she heard more. Elizabeth wondered what she should tell her. If all went as planned she could say whatever she wanted to. She sensed, though, with unusual acuteness, that she must say something that would seem to Beattie final and satisfying if Beattie was ever to lift her cup to her lips. She did not know that what she was sensing was what Beattie meant her to sense and not Beattie's true feeling.

'Well, yes, there *is* something more. Look, maybe I shouldn't interfere in this Beattie but I really think you should know, it seems wrong Bob hasn't told you.'

'Fine. What is it?'

'Bob's asked Dick for a loan to tide the business over till he can raise some more money.'

'How much?'

'Seventy thousand.'

'Seventy thousand?'

'Right.'

'Did Dick tell you this?'

Elizabeth hesitated for a moment, then said, 'Yes.'

'When?'

'Yesterday evening.'

'Has Dick got that sort of money to lend?'

'No. He's got some but not that much. Bob suggested he take out a mortgage on our house.'

'Did he agree?'

'Yes.'

Beattie stood up, on the way lifting the kitten from her lap and dropping her to the ground. She picked up her cup and began to walk from the table.

'Where are you going, Beattie?' Elizabeth got up and followed her. Beattie walked on.

'Give me that. Leave it here.' Elizabeth leant over to take her cup from her. Beattie moved it quickly out of her reach. Elizabeth laughed and said, 'I'll keep it here on the table till you come out again.'

'I'm not coming out again.'

'There's more I can tell you.'

Beattie stopped walking.

'Come and sit down again, Beattie.' Elizabeth reached again for the cup: Beattie again kept it away from her. She gave the impression that she was determined at all costs to hang onto it. Why on earth was she doing that? Elizabeth suddenly suspected that she had guessed everything. My God, she must have done. She was keeping the drink on purpose because she knew it was spiked. She meant to keep it as evidence. She meant to go to the police to accuse Elizabeth of attempting to murder her.

Elizabeth collided with Beattie, ostensibly in turning to go back to her chair, and knocked the cup out of her hand with her arm. It fell and broke and the brown liquid spread rapidly over the stones.

'Oh, my God, I'm so sorry.'

'You did that on purpose.'

'I didn't, Beattie.' Elizabeth touched Beattie's arm. Beattie snatched it away as though scalded.

'Yes, you did.'

The two women stared into each other's eyes. Elizabeth could see now, with perfect clarity, that Beattie guessed everything. Beattie began again to walk fast to the house.

'Where you going, Beattie?' Elizabeth followed her.

Beattie ignored the words and went fast round the side of the building. Elizabeth kept following her. Beattie started to run: Elizabeth ran after her. She must persuade her she was mistaken. But Beattie reached the front door, opened it, leapt over the threshold and slammed the door shut.

Elizabeth discovered on trying to open it that it had been locked.

'Beattie, Beattie,' she called. 'I have to talk to you.'

There was no answer. Elizabeth walked round the house and tried all the windows. They were every one firmly closed. She saw Beattie reach one of them just before she did and lock it.

Elizabeth drove home fast. She was thinking fast. Beattie knew now. She would phone Bob. She must be disposed of as quickly as possible in a manner that could not conceivably implicate Elizabeth Andersen.

The first part of her plan came to her quickly. The second part took longer. It occurred to her only when she thought hard about what Beattie was likely to do with the rest of her day and remembered her saying that she always took Melly for a swim after school. She also recalled Beattie saying that she always parked in the tiny town of New Monmouth and walked to the beach.

As soon as Elizabeth got home she rang Matthew. With the strongest reluctance, after a great deal of persuasion, he agreed to her plan. She was sure he would not have done so had she not been seized by a sudden, inspired remembrance. It came to her while she was talking to him. She saw in her mind's eye a yellow cotton scarf with red spots, tied round a small, thin neck under a pretty ten-year-old face. She had seen it once; she had no idea what had become of it. It might have sunk into mud or floated to sea. It might, even now, be carefully folded in the closet of a still-grieving mother.

She knew it was not what he had used when he strangled her. The news reports had mentioned a piece of bent wire.

She described the scarf with red spots. He remembered it. She had it, she said. She had found it in Erikson's flat and had taken a fancy to it and taken it with her.

At first he had not seemed to believe her. But when she described finding it on the beige sitting-room chair and slipping it into her purse and later putting it away in a drawer in her bedroom, he had appeared convinced that she might be telling the truth after all.

He asked why she had not told him this when she visited him. She said she had forgotten about it. After all, it had been some time ago. She claimed she had come across the scarf again just this morning.

She knew he still could not gauge for sure whether she was telling the truth but did not dare take a chance.

Chapter
Eleven

BEATTIE put down the phone but just missed the receiver. The handset clattered noisily onto the table. She made another, this time successful, attempt to get it in place. She was shaking all over, as she had when she climbed down from the diving board. She walked slowly across to the sofa, sat down and put her head in her hands.

She had phoned Bob's direct line and got his answering machine. Then she had tried the general office number but got no reply. Everyone must be out for the lunch hour. She had called Bob's personal number again and left a long message, telling him all that had happened and asking him to drive up right away. Despite her fury with Bob over his deception of her and, she strongly suspected, himself, she needed him with her.

She felt she could talk openly on the machine since no one but Bob was likely to listen to it.

She now thought hard about what she should do. Her instinct was to stay in the house, with the doors and windows all locked. But she had to go and fetch Melly from school. She had promised her that morning that she would as always take her to the beach for a swim. Of course she could ask Barbara to fetch her, saying she felt ill. But on the other hand what could Elizabeth do to her outside, in public, with people around? She had just told Bob in her message that she and Melly would be at the beach soon after three-thirty. She felt, however irrationally, that they would be safe once he was with them. Of course he might not be convinced by her message. He might not come. But he must come, he must come. She could not be alone in the house with Melly all night. If he stayed down in the City they would both go to Barbara's.

She leaned against the arm of the sofa, her neck bowed, her hands over her eyes.

She felt she had no idea whether he would respond to her call. She felt she now knew him much better than before all this had happened and yet she somehow no longer knew him at all.

But what to do now? She lowered her hands and looked up. Beattie had heard Elizabeth drive away from the house without lingering. She could not have tampered with her car. How else could she immediately endanger her?

Beattie got up and walked slowly, still shaking though now not as violently, to the kitchen. The packet of Ling's Pekinese stood on the table. She wrapped it in a cellophane bag and put it away. Her thoughts turned to Elizabeth's tale of Bob's borrowing money from Dick. She did not doubt it was true. What purpose would Elizabeth have had in making it up? She felt an anger with Bob as she thought of this beyond any anger she had felt before in her life. If the business went under Dick would lose all his money. He would lose his much beloved house and perhaps even his

116

practice. Wayne would desert him once he no longer had capital. Bob would have ruined him.

Beattie was completely convinced that Dick had played no part in and knew nothing of Elizabeth's efforts to kill her.

At the same time she had no doubt that Elizabeth had meant her to die that morning. She was sure she had poisoned her tea. Or at least drugged it. She may have meant to knock her unconscious and then dispose of her so that her death would seem to be suicide.

And what would Bob have thought then?

Beattie took the teapot from the table and carried it across to the sink. She tossed out the dregs.

Of course, if Elizabeth had done the job skilfully, if she had, for example, heaved her over the patio wall so that it looked as though she had jumped, Bob might not have suspected. He might really have believed she had killed herself. He might have known her so little as to assume that on somehow discovering the truth about the state of the business she had despaired. He might have blamed himself for not telling the truth and letting her hear it from others. But not for long. Bob would, she told herself, have decided before her body was cold that her despair was inevitable.

Beattie had discovered at last the identity of that shadow in Bob that she had observed when she first met him. It was a capacity for a self-deceit which when occasion requires permits ruthlessness.

She felt now she could no longer love him. Once all this was over they would part. She would take Melly back home to England.

Beattie tried calling Bob again several times but each time reached the machine. Twice she rang the general office number and the second time got his secretary. She said he had come in after lunch but had immediately gone out again. She did not know where. She did not know whether he had listened first to his messages.

Chapter
Twelve

*D*ICK placed his title deeds back in the safe, shut the door
and turned the knob till it locked. He straightened his
shoulders, brought his head up and back and drew in a long
breath. He lowered his head and turned it to the right, then
the left, breathing out. He rotated it, causing a series of clicks
and squeaks at the base of his skull. He scratched an ear
vigorously and then went to his desk and sat down.

He was alone in the office. Wayne was out on a job; the
secretaries were taking their lunch hour. Dick stretched his
legs out in front of him, keeping his back straight, and
thought over what he had done.

He had yesterday given Bob a cheque for forty thousand
dollars. His bank manager today had made no difficulties
about granting a mortgage for thirty thousand. That money

would come through in a week and he would at once hand it over.

For the first time for months he felt safe. He had bought himself peace of mind.

It was obvious to Dick that Elizabeth was extremely attracted to Bob. He was almost as certain that Bob reciprocated the feeling. After all, if Elizabeth wanted to, he believed, she could make any man love her.

Dick remembered that evening together, after Wayne had first introduced them: the elation he tried so hard to hide when she agreed to go out to dinner; his fear and euphoria as she sat opposite him, so amazingly beautiful, those eyes of hers the biggest and bluest he had ever looked into. It was though he had then entered a dream he had never emerged from. He was her captive still, five years later, though they disagreed on so much and there was often coldness and silence between them.

He could not say he was happy. The two of them seemed not to have grown any closer. She seemed if anything more distant, more unknown than when he first met her. Sometimes she seemed so much a stranger it was hard for him to believe that the marriage had happened and he was really her husband.

But he still loved her passionately.

He had felt afraid for some months that she and Bob would run off together. But this would be impossible, he believed, now that Bob was so deeply in his debt, financially and emotionally.

Chapter Thirteen

*E*LIZABETH reached Lake Tocahoe beach at about two o'clock. The parking area was as always, at that time of day, very full. But she was able to wedge her little Toyota into a small space between two larger cars.

She squeezed out, carrying her towel and her beach bag. The heat grasped her again like a huge, sweaty fist. She relaxed her tummy and straightened up to full height. Holding the bag in her hand, carrying her bright-coloured towel, neatly folded, over her shoulder, keeping her posture erect and with her best social smile already in place, she walked over the rough, stony ground between the closely-packed rows of cars to the open gate, in a tall wire fence, which led to the beach. She was full of the fear of discovery. She always carried this fear: today it had gained a new force. It was not now something buried deep, almost forgotten: it was near to the surface. It was in danger of slithering out through her mouth or her eyes.

She slowed her pace slightly as she approached the gap in the fence. She adjusted and weakened her smile a little so that it would not look fixed. Then she passed through the wide space onto the enclosed, grassy expanse gently rising from the strip of yellow-grey sand rising out of greeny-grey water.

The young woman in charge of the beach, known to Elizabeth only by sight, was lying on her stomach and elbows looking up at her over the top of her sunglasses, which had slid down her nose. Elizabeth gave a nod and a greeting, which the woman returned. For a second Elizabeth felt convinced that the woman was staring suspiciously. But almost at once she returned to the book she was reading. Elizabeth walked on, glancing about among the people crowding the area for a space that was large enough for her to spread out her towel. She needed to be as close as she could to the fence. She needed to be able to see Matthew's car when it drove past. Only then would she know if the plan had succeeded.

She knew that Matthew was seated in his car in the lay-by on the road from New Monmouth. She had driven that way, en route to the beach, to check that he had arrived. The road was sharp-curving and narrow, with a high stone bank on one side and a steep drop on the other.

If all went according to plan Elizabeth would see the big black Ford in about half an hour. It would go past at great speed. If the plan had not worked the car would slow down and Erikson would look round, through the car window, at the beach; then drive on slowly.

Everywhere she looked there were people. Many of them Elizabeth knew. But she could not tell them apart. She saw only indistinguishable bits of humanity. Faces smiled and arms waved and voices called 'Hi' and 'How are you?'. She smiled and waved and called back but she did not know what she said or to whom she was saying it.

She spotted a space, of sufficient length and breadth for her towel, towards the back of the grassy expanse. It was in the sun: she would have much preferred shade. But there was no place else she could go that was near enough to the fence. She walked slowly towards it, still holding herself very tall. With slow, deliberate movements, as though afraid of making some clumsy mistake, she sat down and arranged her limbs, one stretched out before her, one bent in the unmet half of a cross-legged position. The sole of her foot faced her thigh; her knee was high off the ground. She was not specially supple. She never had been, even as a young child. She had not been good at gymnastics or dancing. She had all her life felt self-conscious when in physical motion and sometimes even at rest. She knew she lacked grace.

She took her suntan lotion and her paperback book out of the beach bag and put them down next to her.

A few moments later she rose again, holding the beach bag, to walk to the changing room.

A youngish man appeared in front of her, smiling and exclaiming. Elizabeth smiled and spoke in reply, automatically, without seeing his face or remembering his name. She left him with a sideways bend of the head, the intense smile remaining till, out of his sight, it subsided to the vaguer one that had been on her face before he had approached her.

She reached the Ladies' changing room, which was up some steps on the first floor of a small wooden hut, above the Men's changing room and the Lost and Found area. In one of the lavatories she took off her suntop and shorts. She had her swimsuit on underneath. She wore her one-piece suit, not her bikini. She felt it to be altogether more suitable for the staring eyes at the beach. She crammed her clothes into the beach bag. Then she went out into the communal changing room, which happened to be at that moment empty, and turned to the mirror. Her blue eyes stared back at her. She quickly fished her comb and lipstick out of the beach bag and with a few rapid motions, glancing into the mirror only as necessary, combed her hair and applied some more lipstick.

When she was on the way back to her towel she passed

an old man and half noticed that his white skin that was dotted with a great many moles and brown patches but, though she had known him a great many years, she could not have said who he was. He and Elizabeth smiled and exchanged a few words of greeting, then passed by.

Elizabeth lay for a while stretched out, face down. The front of her body, which, with all the rest of her, she had smeared well with suntan lotion, felt sticky. The sun's heat bore into her. Her breathing, for someone lying prone and not moving a muscle, came hard, fast and shallow.

She did not experience the anxiety she was feeling as a churning or butterflies but as a tension all through her. Her flesh seemed vulnerable as the body feels vulnerable when one is ill and weak or unusually cold. It was as though, if anyone touched her, she would feel sharp, intense pain.

She went over the plan in her mind: then she sat up abruptly, reached for her book, lay back down, on an elbow, and opened at the page she had reached, where she had turned down the corner.

For a few minutes she tried to read the words on the page. They were not difficult words. They were written to be understood with only a part of the mind. But they could have been inscribed in Dutch or Chinese for all the sense she could make of them.

She checked the time. She had at least half an hour before the car could come past. Beattie picked up Melly from school at three-thirty; they would reach New Monmouth five minutes later. It would take three or four minutes to walk to where Matthew was parked. She put down the book and took off her wristwatch. She placed them both under her beach bag. Then she took out her bathing cap and stretched it over her head. She made sure she had tucked in every last hair. She stood up. Then she walked slowly, avoiding treading on the sunbathers and their belongings strewn over the grass, to the greeny-grey water.

There was a large rock on one side of the beach, beyond the roped-off area watched by the lifeguard. She climbed onto it, walked to the end and dived in.

124

The water was wonderfully cool. She swam quickly and strongly towards the lake's centre.

She was an excellent swimmer. She had been taught a stylish breaststroke and crawl as a child. She took a long, slow breath each time she brought her head and right arm up out of the water, then, as her head went under again, her eyes open, she slowly exhaled.

When she was way out in the lake she slowed her pace. She swam in a more leisurely manner for a few hundred yards. Then she moved in a half-circle and looked back to where she had come from. The beach was almost invisible against the low, purple-green hills. The people were specks. She swam back round to face the lake's centre.

The water here was its deepest and cleanest. Its texture was different from how it was near the shore. It was smoother and silkier. The land seemed very far off. Above, the sun shone with fierce heat in the huge blue cavern of sky, but without power now to hurt her.

She moved almost noiselessly, doing her best breast-stroke. She pushed her arms and kicked her legs without causing the tiniest splash. Someone had said once that the water was Elizabeth's element. She had understood the words merely to signify that she swam very well. But the speaker – a man who admired her – in truth meant that Elizabeth, like some amphibious creature, took on a grace in the water that she was lacking on land.

As she swam slowly down the middle part of the lake the whole world became nothing but water and sky. For a brief moment or two she forgot everything. She forgot the very existence of her own flesh and being. She felt some-thing like peace.

She lifted an arm and straightened it and began to flip-flop her legs as she changed her stroke back to the crawl. She put her head under water, eyes open, just as she had been taught more than twenty years earlier. The cool liquid held and caressed her.

She made a sudden decision to dive under and stay under for as long as she could. First she surfaced again and inhaled as much air as would go into her lungs. Then she dived down two or three feet.

She could not quite see to the bottom. The water was cleaner out here but not clean enough for a view all the way down. She envisioned clear ocean brine of a crystalline blue, a blue that seemed purified sky. She saw in her memory the distant but distinct grey and green ocean floor.

She saw, with an extraordinary clarity as though the years had dissolved and she was again ten years old, a man swimming beside her. They were competing. They were to see who could stay under longest.

Elizabeth's lungs began to feel strain: she kept under for another few moments: then she slid up to the surface and gasped in mouthfuls of air.

They swam back to the shore. He was praising her, telling her she was an expert, a champion, that she had the best pair of lungs he had known in a child, that he was tremendously proud of her, that she would win medals. She seemed to glow warmly, though her body was cool in cool water. She beamed at him across the few inches between them of the dark, sun-sprinkled surface. Her leg had accidentally brushed against his: she did not mind the touch in the least: it seemed part, with their talking and laughter, of their closeness and happiness.

On the beach she tore off her swimming cap and jumped with elation and stood on her tiptoes and put her arms round his neck and pulled him down towards her to kiss him on his thin cheeks. His pale blue eyes, free of their glasses and bright from the swim, had changed their expression to one that made her feel she had done something wrong. But the expression was not of displeasure. It was oddly, unusually serious. He had kissed her quickly and straightened up and she had let go. Then he had taken her forearm and squeezed it. He looked, still, strangely solemn.

'We'll go home now.'

'Why, what is it? Is something the matter?'

'No, nothing's the matter, dear. I have to cook the dinner for us, remember. There's no Mom to do it.'

'I'm gonna change into my new clothes when we get back.'

'Sure. I'd like to see them on you.'

'Maybe I'll try them all on and then I'll decide which to wear. She left me two T-shirts and a dress and two pairs of jeans. She bought them all from the store where she works. She gets them half-price but it was real nice of her anyway.'

'She's always been one for gifts when she feels guilty.'

'Why does she feel guilty?'

'Well, maybe she doesn't, who knows. But mothers do sometimes when they go away on a trip leaving their children. Some mothers.'

'I thought it was kind of her, buying those clothes.'

'Yeah, I suppose it was.'

'She says I'll look great in them. She's always paying me compliments.'

'You deserve them.'

'She says I'm the best-looking girl in the school.'

'It's no more than the truth.'

They walked over the sand, deserted apart from themselves and a small group a hundred yards off, towards the hut where their clothes were.

The day had been one of the best Elizabeth had spent in her life. He had smiled and talked to her with unfailing kindness; he had shown he was proud of her. He had given her his undivided attention. He had never once glanced at a paper or book or turned on the radio or looked bored or abstracted. He seemed to share her excitement at their being alone together.

Her mother had left after breakfast that morning on a business trip. He was to look after her for a week. She had never felt cared for like this. She had never felt this kind of happiness.

'You go on in and change first,' he said. 'I'll wait here. I'll go in when you've finished.'

They came home to the small house on the long high street, with woods at the back sloping away to the shore. She and her mother and brother had moved there a few months before and this man had joined them quite soon. Her mother had found a job in the area: a good job in a shop. She was one of the people who chose what clothes it should buy. She had to go away now to the fashion shows in the East. Elizabeth had wanted to go with her but she had said she could not take time off from her school.

This new man in their lives was planning to buy some kind of a store in the area and to continue to live with them.

Her brother, much older than she was, had, a few days before, gone off to college.

They knew nobody in the street or the town. They knew nobody in the whole State. No one whose face or voice was familiar to them was nearer than two thousand miles eastward over the continent.

Elizabeth had gone upstairs to take her new items of clothing out of the wardrobe and try them on one by one. He went to the kitchen to start making dinner.

After a while he called up to her to say it was ready. She came down in a pair of tight-fitting blue jeans and a red, sleeveless T-shirt.

'Why, that's attractive. A real eye-catching outfit.'

His eyes were most certainly caught. They made her think as he gazed at her of two marbles submerged under water.

At dinner she had taken his hand and said, 'I do love you. Mom's kind to me but she's so *busy*, she never does anything with me like you do, she's always at work or out, going places.' She added after a moment or two, with sudden anger and pain, 'She's not always kind.'

'I love you too, Lizzie.' He smiled at her kindly. 'I love taking you places and doing things with you.'

She squeezed his hand hard.

Later they watched television and at ten o'clock he told her to go up to bed. He said he would come up in a little while to say goodnight.

He came up as promised.

He sat on her bed and held her hand and then stroked her arm. He talked to her about her swimming and the new school she was starting. He gazed at her with a look in his eyes which seemed kind at first but then gradually changed. It became strange and baffling. He fell silent.

'What is it? What's wrong?'

'There's nothing wrong. Here, come closer. Come up closer.' He pulled her towards him.

And then he had undone the buttons of his trousers and pulled out the horrible, red, raw-looking thing, shaped like a huge sausage with a funny cleft end.

He said she should touch it.

She had no choice. She had no power of will. She felt paralysed. She wanted to jump out of bed and run but her legs would not move. And there was nowhere to run to. She made no sound but inside she was screaming.

There seemed blackness all round her. The world had turned into violence.

He did not touch her, that night, beyond stroking her arm to the shoulder. But he made her touch and fondle that thing till liquid streamed out of it over her bedclothes.

She quietly cried when that happened. He wiped away her tears, saying nothing but 'Don't cry, don't cry.' Inside herself she was still screaming.

She did not know if what she was doing would be thought of by other people as wrong. She felt afraid that if they knew they would blame her. Yet she felt afraid too that to say no or push him away was just as wrong, perhaps more so. She saw blackness and violence everywhere.

The second night he had come to her room he had touched her all over. When his hand was between her legs, on the slit, he had told her to stroke and fondle him in the same way as the evening before. The liquid this time had streamed onto her legs.

The third night he had got right into her bed instead of lying on top of it. He had stroked her body and arms and then touched the slit between her legs with his hand and then he had put the horrible thing into it. He pushed it further and further till she felt she would burst apart down the middle. He caused her the most intense pain she had known in her life. This time she had screamed out loud and not just inside her own head and he had put his hand over her mouth and said 'Ssshhh, Sssshhh', in a voice that made him sound as though he was tired. He said nothing else after that. Later he got out of bed and silently went from the room.

His act – not at once but in its repetitions and gradual effects – ossified her still-warm, living heart.

After that time he came to her room nearly every night for the two and a half years he lived with her and her mother. She had hoped that when Mom returned from her trip he would stop coming but he had simply come later on in the night when her mother and herself gone to bed. Her brother, when he came home on vacation, saw and knew nothing.

He told her that if she told her mother, or anyone, what they did, he would be sent to prison and she to a special boarding school where she would not see him or her mother till she was allowed out, many years later, when she grew up.

In the daytime he was still her kind uncle.

Often she was asleep when Matthew came to her room. He would wake her as he climbed into bed. Often he woke her from a terrible dream. But the waking was not a relief. The reality was more terrible even than any terrible dream.

Chapter
Fourteen

*E*LIZABETH returned to her towel, spread out on the grass. She took her watch out of her bag. The time was a quarter past three. She smeared on more suntan lotion. Then she lay down on her front, her head turned to the fence, her eyes on the road. She had a clear view past the parked cars, since the grass rose a little to the fenced-off area.

No Ford appeared. After twenty minutes she sat up and peered across at the parking lot but then lay back down again. After three quarters of an hour she stood up. She looked all round her. The crowd was spread as thickly as ever over the grass and the sand. There were no cars arriving or leaving or passing beyond the tall wire fence. She saw in her mind, as she had repeatedly during that day since she phoned Matthew, two figures lying dead in the road.

But then something half-glimpsed over the beach in the other direction made her turn her gaze further behind her, towards the road that ran along at the back of the fenced-in grass area. The effect on her was as of seeing two ghosts. The figures were instantly recognisable, yet they could not really be there — her eyes must be tricking her. And yet, as she stared, they remained, they came closer.

There were Beattie and Melly walking onto the road from a gap in the trees she had never before been aware of. Beattie was still wearing the suntop and skirt she had had on that morning. Melly was in a navy blue T-shirt with some short word written across it that she could not read at this distance.

She lay down again quickly and turned her head face down to the towel.

Her bewilderment and confusion and fear made her again doubt her own eyesight. She turned her head, watching the road. They came into view: she faced the other way quickly. These were no ghosts. Beattie must have discovered her plan; she had purposely come to the beach by some other route than the road. But how could she have found out? And by what other route? Elizabeth knew after thinking a moment or two that there was no conceivable means by which Beattie could have discovered what she intended. She had told no one but Matthew. She must have walked some other way, down some trail Elizabeth had not known about, just because she preferred to. It was that strange, absurd English liking for a walk for the sake of it. Elizabeth suddenly remembered that a private road led from New Monmouth. She had never previously known or even wondered where it emerged. She realised now that of course it must come out at that gap in the trees, where she had seen them.

She half raised herself on her elbow and peered over the beach. They were nowhere in sight. She raised herself further. Suddenly she spotted Beattie bent over, at the far end of the grassy expanse, spreading a towel. Then she saw Melly with her arms high, pulling her shirt up over her head.

Elizabeth got up, quickly pulled her suntop and shorts on over her swimsuit, pushed her feet into her sandals, gathered her things up and, looking straight ahead of her and speaking to no one, left the beach. She got into her car and drove off down the road towards New Monmouth.

In the parked Ford, in the lay-by from which he had a clear view down the road to the next curve, a hundred yards on, Matthew waited. They would surely be along soon. They should have passed half an hour ago.

The road was narrow, with a high bank on one side, a steep drop on the other. Cars came along it infrequently. New Monmouth was so small a town as to be merely a village. It had one row of shops, which included a drugstore, a barber's, a sandwich bar and Elizabeth's gallery. The road Matthew was waiting on was not a main thoroughfare. Most people came to the beach from the other direction. But the cars that did come drove very fast. It was a dangerous road for pedestrians.

Since he had waited there had been no pedestrians.

There had seemed no choice for Matthew but to agree to Elizabeth's plan. She had convinced him of her determination to tell all she knew to Wayne or the police if he did not. On the phone she had sounded as he had never heard her before. She had shown the desperation of someone with nothing to lose. He believed completely that her threats this time were genuine. More significant still was that she claimed to have evidence. He did not know for certain whether she truly had in her possession that yellow scarf with red spots. But he believed it was possible. He had seen it in his mind, as she spoke, knotted round the slim neck. The girl had not had it on that last time he was with her. It was possible, as Elizabeth claimed, that it had been left on a chair in the sitting room. It was possible that Elizabeth had taken it that day she came to the apartment after the girl had been with him.

That had been the worst possible luck. If Elizabeth had been a minute earlier or later she would not have met his young companion coming out through his door to the corridor.

He was expecting them, moment by moment. They would come walking into his angle of vision from the New Monmouth direction. He could not fail to know them when they appeared. The woman would be slim and dark and the girl would be tall for her age and stockily built.

He was beginning to find the waiting well-nigh unbearable. He was beginning seriously to want to abandon it, to start the engine and drive off back to the City, regardless of consequences. But each time he reached the point in his thoughts when he imagined those consequences he knew again he was trapped. He was certain that one way or another he would not live to come out of gaol.

More time passed and no one walked into his sight. He felt almost unbearably hot though he had opened both windows. When he felt in the pack for another cigarette he found he had finished them all. He crumpled the paper and pressed it into the ashtray.

Only a very few vehicles went past. He began to grow angry. He felt a hatred for Elizabeth of a violence such as he had never felt before in his life.

Then a car drove up from behind him and braked. The very person of whom he was at that moment thinking with loathing was next to him. She slid down her window. The brilliant blue eyes he had seen in his mind were looking straight in at him. She had not switched off the engine.

'They won't be coming this way now. I can't take time to explain. I don't want to be seen here. When I've gone turn the car around and keep waiting. They'll be coming along soon from the other direction.'

She slid up her window, pulled away and drove off down the road fast.

Matthew had said nothing. He sat for a while, considering, searching again in his mind for an alternative course. But at last, his anger and fear once more vanquished by greater fear, he started the engine, pulled the car out in the road, turned around and then drove back into the lay-by. He now faced in the direction that led to the lake. The road stretched in front of him for about a hundred yards to the next bend. The steep incline rose up on his right: across the road, on his left, was the drop to the stream. If a car came along when they approached he could turn round and tail them. He could wait till the best moment. If a car arrived at the critical stage he would be gone before it could stop him.

Chapter Fifteen

*E*LIZABETH turned into the main street of the village and parked in front of the short row of shops. She got out and walked the few steps to the pharmacy, where she bought another tube of suntan lotion and a packet of Kleenex. She wanted to establish a reason for walking here. She then walked the few yards to her gallery. She let herself in and went through to the office.

Near the phone at the back of the room was the New Monmouth phone book.

After some searching she found, in a list under New Monmouth Parks and Facilities, the number of the phone at the beach in the Lost and Found area. She punched the digits.

The voice belonging to the woman with descending sunglasses answered.

'I've an important message for Beattie O'Connor. Please would you get her for me?'

'She just left.'

'Oh, no.'

'Who is this?'

'It's a friend of hers. I've got an important message for her from her husband.'

'Look, she and her daughter went over to Harry's Pizza Hut. You could get her there.'

'Great. Thanks.'

Elizabeth again went through the procedure of phone book and punching the digits. This time, after explaining what Beattie looked like to the pizza-maker who answered, she heard 'Hallo?' in Beattie's unmistakable, slightly 'off', American accent.

Elizabeth raised her voice to a slow, high-pitched quaver.

'Mrs O'Connor? You don't know me. I've got a message for you from your husband. I just saw him in New Monmouth.'

'Who are you?'

'I'm no one you know. I live in Marbury. I'm calling to tell you your husband's in New Monmouth High Street with a flat tyre. I was going on home when I met him changing it and we got talking and he asked me to call you at the beach to tell you to walk there to meet him.'

'How did you know to call me here?'

Elizabeth could not be sure whether Beattie's tone was suspicious or just puzzled.

'I called the beach first and they told me you'd gone across to the Pizza Hut.'

'Well, thanks.'

'He seemed real anxious to see you, honey.'

There was a pause. Elizabeth's stomach was queasy. She felt herself sweating.

Beattie said, 'You've gone to a lot of trouble.'

Her tone was still, to Elizabeth, ambiguous.

'No trouble. I've time on my hands.'

'Still . . .'

'Listen, honey, one other thing, he said to walk along the main road because if he gets the car going he'll come along it and meet you.

There was a pause. Then Beattie said, 'O.K.'

'I have to go now, honey. Bye.'

Elizabeth put down the phone. She felt dizzy almost to fainting. Her stomach was heaving.

Bob drove fast along the curving road. He passed on his right, parked in the road's solitary lay-by, a black Ford. He glimpsed an old man inside, with a thin face and large glasses. The man's expression struck him with particular force. But it was not till later that he tried to work out its significance.

He arrived at the beach. There was no space in the parking lot. After parking illegally on the road just before the small bridge crossing the stream, he walked to the fence. His wife and daughter were not anywhere on the grass or sand or in the water at the edge of the lake. He was sure they had not swum out to the raft. Beattie never did that with Melly. She liked only to do it alone.

Bob turned away, intending to cross to the Pizza Hut. But then he remembered that Beattie claimed always to walk to the beach along the private road by the stream. He at once set off towards it, round the back of the fenced-in area. He suddenly spotted a car he was almost sure was Elizabeth's. It seemed strange that he had not seen Elizabeth. Was she somewhere with Beattie and Melly? Had she taken them somewhere? But how could she, when her car was still here?

He found the entrance to the dirt road: Beattie had pointed it out to him once. That had been soon after she first told him of walking that way. He had never before noticed that gap in the trees.

The browny-orange track stretched ahead, the fast-running stream on its left, dense woods on the right. He walked quickly. The place seemed odd and silent and solitary. It appeared a quite different country, with its own laws and history. He understood now its attraction for Beattie.

When she first told Bob she had walked there he was surprised. He had said surely she had known that dirt road was private. She had asked why that should matter since she was doing no harm. He had explained that in his country no one but the owners of land, or those to whom they give their permission, are allowed to walk on it, even on roadways. She might well have been confronted by an angry proprieter armed with a shotgun. Beattie had expressed amazement and strong indignation.

He had realised that this was the first time since she had come to this country that Beattie had grasped fully the distinction between New and Old World concepts of ownership of land. Her outrage seemed to Bob rather baffling but had not lessened with time.

Defiantly, as a matter of principle as well as convenience, she had gone on using the private road whenever she, or she and Melly, walked to the beach from New Monmouth. She knew the owners might one day return and discover them. This risk did not alarm her. Beattie was not generally much burdened by apprehension or fear. Such feelings were perhaps even converted at some deep level into something pleasurable and gratifying. Bob often pointed out to her that she seemed to enjoy taking risks.

Mother and daughter walked along the private road every day after school. The beach parking lot was full by mid-afternoon and Beattie preferred to leave the car in the village. The main road was shorter than the private one but much less pleasant and also quite dangerous. Cars were infrequent but when they came they came fast. The banks on each side – on the one hand rock and concrete supporting a vertical incline, on the other a sheer wooded drop – gave no means of escape. A reckless or incompetent driver could kill. This was one risk that Beattie, whatever Bob might say about her liking for danger, had no wish whatsoever to take.

In any case, she had told Bob, that track through the woods along by the stream had a solitude and mystery she could not resist.

Bob now felt a great strangeness in walking in new territory, with a new fear. When a few hours earlier he had heard Beattie telling her tale, in a voice distorted a little by a crackling on the answering machine tape, a terror had filled him surpassing anything he had felt in his life.

'She knocked the cup out of my hand. She knew I knew.'

He had at first not quite caught the words. He had played the tape back a few times till he was sure of them.

'She kept on and on that she'd make the tea,' Beattie had said earlier. 'She'd been down to the City on a *Sunday* to buy it. She came up here with it on a Monday morning, when she should have been in the gallery. She was desperate to make it herself, with me out of the kitchen. You've got to believe me, Bob, she poisoned the tea. I left the room for a minute to answer the phone. Actually I changed my mind and came back before answering it but all the same she was alone for a while. That's when she did it.'

Bob did believe her. All Elizabeth's actions seemed so bizarre, so inexplicable in ordinary terms, as to convince him her intentions were evil.

Bob found he was not surprised to discover that Elizabeth was malign. He knew now he had suspected as much all along. But he had not cared to face the suspicion since Elizabeth's attempt to harm Beattie might have been due to anger and hatred – or love – for himself. But he now saw Saturday night's events just as Beattie did. Elizabeth had sent her to dive into a pool she must have known to be empty of water. She had wanted to kill her.

Nothing mattered any longer but the need to protect his wife and his child. The fate of the business, his house, his whole future, now seemed trivial. They could go hang.

He had left at once, after hearing the message, without saying a word to his secretary, and had driven to New

Monmouth in less time than he had ever done the journey before.

The trees shaded the track; the hill rising up on his left, past the stream, threw a still deeper shadow. He walked quickly. He kept on for a considerable distance. He was thinking now of that car in the lay-by. Its presence there seemed more than an oddity: it seemed threatening.

He turned back before reaching the end of the track. If Beattie and Melly were walking this way they would have by now got at least this far.

He said aloud. 'I have to check on that car.'

He almost ran down the rest of the track and out onto the road and back to the parking area. A long look through the fence, at the beach, showed that Beattie and Melly still were not there. He again thought of the Pizza Hut. He decided that despite his urge to go immediately to the parked car it was more logical to look first in the restaurant.

But, as he was on the point of crossing the road, he spotted Elizabeth Andersen's Toyota with its owner now sitting inside it. The engine was switched off. Elizabeth sat quite still, staring ahead of her. He moved back quickly before she could see him. There seemed some strange link between this woman in her car and the glimpsed man in the Ford. They had both the same expression: a look of tense waiting; but with more to it than that. He realised they both looked afraid. It was as though they held some dangerous secret almost too dreadful to bear.

The need to see if the Ford was still there and to speak to that man became overwhelming. He got into his car and set off down the road to New Monmouth.

Elizabeth's feeling of nausea had grown stronger as she drove back to the beach after making the phone call to Beattie. She had reached the Ladies' room just in time. Holding her hair back from her face, she threw up in the lavatory bowl.

Afterwards, when she had washed her face and put on new foundation and lipstick, she walked to her car. She got in and sat for a while. She could not decide what to do. Had Matthew driven past while she was inside? The need to know what had happened was growing. It became irresistible. She started the car and began to back out. But another car was now parked in front of her. She needed to manoeuvre very precisely and carefully to escape but seemed unable to do so. The frustration was almost making her scream.

She flung open the car door, got out and started to walk.

She envisaged Beattie's limp body at the side of the road. She would run back to the beach to report the accident by phone, just like anyone would.

'Mommy, why are we walking this way?'

'It's quicker than down by the stream. We'll meet Daddy sooner.'

'It's not as nice.'

'I know.'

'It's kind of private down there. Like it's all ours.'

'Yeah.'

'Along here you have to watch for cars. Can't we go the other way?'

'Oh, God, Mel, I told you, this is quicker.'

'What's the matter, Mom?'

'Nothing's the matter.'

'You're all jumpy.'

'I'm fine.'

'I hate it when you get jumpy.'

'It's only the heat.'

'Will Daddy come back to the beach with us?'

'I don't know.'

'Will he have his swimming things?'

'I don't know. Let's walk faster.'

Up ahead of them a black Ford was parked in the lay-by.

Two figures were coming quickly towards him, at the right side of the road next to the steep bank of stone. One was a thin woman, in a suntop and skirt, the other a girl in shorts with long, plump legs. She had on a navy blue T-shirt with some large but, at this distance, undecipherable letters printed across it. The two walked almost side by side, the woman slightly ahead of the girl.

He started the engine. He looked around. There were no cars coming in either direction. He released the brake and drove forward. He put his foot hard down on the gas pedal and quickly gained speed.

The girl moved nearer the stone wall. The woman kept to her place in the road, still walking. He could see she was not yet suspicious. A small white Mustang appeared round the bend. Matthew kept straight on but slowed his pace slightly. The woman moved nearer the bank. He passed between her and the other car, slowing down even more, driving with great care for the pedestrians' safety.

He rounded the bend. He could see ahead, at the end of a long, narrow stretch of road, a wide crossing. Beyond this, on the left, was the beach. There was a parking lot next to it jammed full of cars. Opposite was a wooden hut inscribed, in large letters, 'Harry's Pizza'. Matthew stopped at the six-sided, red 'Stop' sign: a car passed in front of him and drew up at the hut. The crossing was now clear: he swung round in a U-turn.

Beattie and Melly were nearing the next bend, a sharp one. They kept well over on the left. No vehicle rounding the curve would expect to encounter pedestrians.

Beattie was beginning to feel weary. Though they were in the shade of the bank on their left she was sweating. Her canvas bag hung heavily, the strap cutting into her shoulder. Luckily Melly seemed not to be tired. She had been refreshed by her swim and the pizza. She looked forward eagerly to seeing her father. Despite Beattie's tiredness they kept walking briskly.

'I can't imagine Daddy mending a flat tyre.'

'He won't be mending the tyre. He'll be changing it.'

Melly laughed.

'I can't imagine that either.'

'Daddy can do things like that if he has to.'

'Why doesn't he take the car to the garage?'

'You can't drive a car when it's got a flat tyre.'

'I hope he'll still be changing it when we get there. I'd like to see him doing it.'

'I hope he'll have finished.'

There was the rumbling of a car coming up from behind. Beattie glanced round. It was that same black Ford. Why was it coming back the way it had gone? The driver had an old man's face, long, with big glasses. The car was close to them now. She and Melly stopped walking and pressed themselves against the high bank. Beattie caught the man's eye. She saw a flicker of fear. Was he tailing them? She expected at any moment the car to slow down and stop.

She felt almost dizzy with relief as it swept on past them round the sharp bend.

Matthew kept going. He knew he could not chance driving at them when they were so near a curve. A car or pedestrian might appear even as he was running them down. After he had rounded the bend another curve was upon him almost at once. But after that the road was straight for a while and widened a little. He drove on for a couple of minutes and then slowed down and braked. He executed a tight three-point turn. Then he came back, stopped in the road and awaited them. He did not switch off the engine.

'Is it much further?'

'A few minutes more.'

'Is it round this next bend?'

'Not quite. But it's not far now.'

'Look, you can see the hills there through the trees.'

'So you can. I've never noticed that before.'

They both stopped walking.

'Aren't they beautiful?'

'Yes, they are.'

'Mommy!' Melly screamed. 'There's a deer! I can see a deer!'

'Where?'

'He's gone now. Oh, gosh.'

'What a pity.'

'Couldn't we go look for him?'

'No. We can't go off the road. There's a drop. Any-way . . .'

'This must be the most beautiful place in the world, Mom. New Dartmouth, I mean.'

'I agree, Mel. I've never been anywhere more beauti-ful.'

They began walking again, keeping close to the stone bank, round the bend.

'Mom, there's that car again.'

Beattie grabbed Melly's shoulder.

Melly said, 'Why's it parked there like that, out in the road?'

'I don't know.'

'It's started moving.'

'Yes.'

'It's going awfully fast.'

'Get over.'

'It's coming right at us.'

'Oh, my God.'

Melly was screaming.

Beattie swung around, desperately scanning the scene for a way of escape. But on the left was the high wall; over the road was the steep drop to the stream. There was nowhere to run to.

Matthew kept pressing as hard as he could on the gas pedal. The woman was turning to look all round and behind her. Her expression was terrified. Her mouth was open. He kept his foot hard down on the pedal. She looked thin and fragile: she would break easily. The girl was nearer the bank, holding onto the woman, a little behind her. Her mouth too was open. The letters on the navy blue T-shirt were almost clear now. The girl stepped back and stumbled a little. Matthew kept pressing hard.

Bob made the right turn into the narrow main road to New Monmouth.

'She knocked the cup out of my hand. She knew I knew.' He heard the words again in his head, as they were on the tape, distorted by crackling.

The lay-by was beyond the next bend. As he swung round it he saw the black Ford was now gone. He drove on quickly; he rounded a second bend, then a third. He saw a car heading his way. He recognised it. At the same moment he saw Beattie and Melly right in its path. It was driving straight at them. He pressed the gas pedal down to the floor and swerved hard left between them and the car, straight at the wall. The grey stones grew huge as he jammed his foot with all his strength on the brake.

As Matthew read the word 'Yale' it was eclipsed. There was a screeching of brakes and, as he swerved left, a screaming of metal. He hurtled on at top speed down the road. He realised he must have torn off the other car's bumper and might still be trailing it. He kept going; he swept round the curve.

A woman was walking towards him on the right side of the road by the wall. She was tall and a little ungainly. A lock of hair had fallen out of place over one eyebrow. Her eyes were bright blue. They caught and held his as though with mesmeric power. With a surge of fury and despair he drove straight towards them.

It took Elizabeth only a moment to realise what Matthew intended. She wanted to run but her legs would not move. She was screaming but no sound came from her lips. His big, pale, staring eyes behind the windscreen grew larger and larger. Her whole being was gripped by an unsurpassable horror as she knew beyond doubt she had ahead of her less than a moment of life.

She was hurled through the air into a deep lake of pain. Its waters engulfed her.

She was swimming. She was still underwater but she needed no air. The brine was a pure and crystalline blue.

Beattie wrenched open the car door. Behind her Melly was crying. He sat quite still, slumped forward.

'Bob!' She pulled at his shoulder but his weight was too great for her. For the first time in her life since earliest childhood a sound came from her that was free from restraint. It was a howl of unbearable anguish.

Melly was pulling at her from behind, calling 'Mommy, Mommy', her voice filled with whimpering terror.

Bob raised his head a fraction and looked at Beattie, his eyes blank with shock.

'You're alive!'

She threw her arms round his neck. They hugged with a passion surpassing anything either had previously known.

A moment later Beattie moved a little and with her arm swept Melly into her parents' embrace. For a long while they all three clung together.

Chapter
Sixteen

*E*VERYONE assumed that Elizabeth's death was an accident. A hit and run driver had done it. Some who had seen her shortly before on the beach had thought she seemed distant and strange. Some thought she had had a premonition of death. But where she was heading on foot was also a mystery and always would be so.

Bob told the story to the police, of the parked Ford and the attempt by the driver to take Beattie's life. They assumed the man had been drunk or mad. In any case, they believed he was unknown to either of the two women and the girl he had so nearly killed.

Bob and Beattie knew better. They now knew it was Elizabeth who had made that phone call to Beattie, in order to lure her onto the road. But there seemed no point in telling the story. They had no evidence that Elizabeth was a psychopath or that she had wanted Beattie to die.

They never knew who Elizabeth's accomplice was, or why he had killed her.

The car was towed away and the police took them to the station, to sign a statement.

Bob had found that he was unharmed except for a swelling, purple bruise on his forehead. But he was so shaken that he could scarcely keep hold of his pen as he scribbled his signature.

Dick arrived while they were still there. He nodded to Bob, seeming hardly to see him. He stared at Beattie, wild-eyed. His round face was very white, his neck aflame with a terrible rash.

'I can't believe it,' he kept saying.

'I'm so sorry, Dick. I'm dreadfully sorry.'

She really did feel great sorrow for him. Dick had never had the chance to be happy in his marriage but now that his wife was dead he was distracted with grief.

Dick's eyes filled with tears. He jerked his shoulders back, shaking his head.

'Couldn't she have moved out of the way? Couldn't she *see* the car?'

'They think it must have been either a drunk or a maniac who did it deliberately. It would have happened very quickly. She wouldn't have felt any pain.'

Dick's expression was agonised. He jerked his head sideways and blinked away a tear.

'She was always very fond of you, Beattie. She always wanted to get to be closer friends.'

'Mmmm.'

'I can't believe it's happened. I can't believe she's dead.'

'I'll come and see you tomorrow.'

'Please do. Please.'

'God arranged for me to be there.'

'No. You should take the credit, Bob.'

'It was extraordinary that I turned that bend then.'

'It was brilliant timing.'

Bob pulled her closer.

She asked, 'Did you think you'd die in the crash?'

'Sure.'

She leant her head on his shoulder and he hugged her even more closely.

A little later Beattie said, 'Why did she hate me so much?'

'Darling, she was obviously some sort of psychopath.'

'But why me? Why did she want to kill *me*?'

'She tried to seduce me once.'

'You never told me.'

'She didn't succeed.'

'So that was her reason.'

That evening, Bob told Beattie everything there was to tell about the state of the business. The situation was as hopeless as she had suspected. He had deluded both her and himself for weeks, if not months.

They were standing outside on the patio. They walked to the patio wall and leant against it, gazing over the late evening landscape. Saturday's sliver of moon had broadened a little. There were a great many stars. There was just enough light for them to make out the uneven, dark shape of the forest off to the left. The black, linked silhouettes of the branches, webbed with leaves, scarcely moved. Now and then clumps of long fingers, pointing out to infinity, bent slowly earthwards a fraction, then as slowly returned.

Beattie looked towards the Andersens' chimney stack, now invisible.

'Poor Dick.'

'Will you really go and see him tomorrow?'

'We should both go.'

'Yeah, O.K.'

'You have to give back the loan.'

'Do I?'

'Bob . . .'

'Yes, I do.'

'You've got to start bankruptcy proceedings.'

'I know.'

'Promise.'

'I promise.'

Beattie too made a promise.

She knew now what the shadow was in Bob's nature but it had been dispelled by the sunlight. Bob had knowingly, purposely risked his own life for hers. And as a result, in the illumination of gratitude, she had more clearly than ever before seen her own shadow. It was as dark as her husband's. But she too now would let in some light.

She did not speak her own promise aloud. He would never know of it. But in time he would see its results. She would not bear him a brood but she would give him the child she believed, and hoped, she was carrying.

They sat for some time out in the warm, dark evening air discussing present and future.

There was no denying the bleakness. They would lose the house and the land and all their possessions. They would have to go back to the City to live. Beattie had hoped when they moved she had left it for ever. And she was well aware of the almost bottomless depths of Bob's disappointment. She sensed the weight of depression that surely would last for a very long time.

Nothing in the time that was coming – least of all the carrying out of her new resolution – would be straightforward or easy.

But they were still young. They had the strength to start again. They would survive. And when they had made enough money they would return to this landscape.

Beattie knew now that it was her home. She had no other. She had nearly died here, she had suffered anguish and terror, but the sense of belonging remained with her still. It would never be lost. She had become one with these mountains and forests and lakes.

She was never to know that their beauty and mystery had, that day, saved her life.

152